1

You shouldn't chase after the past
or place expectations on the future.
What is past
is left behind.
The future
is as yet unreached.
Whatever quality is present
you clearly see right there,
right there.

from Bhaddekaratta Sutta, Majjhima Nikaya 131 (An
Auspicious Day)

Rutherford Nature Preserve and Open-Air Museum
Jonah Bell Dig Site
Outside Huntsville, Alabama

Thursday, January 2nd, just after sunrise

D avina Truth Jones stifled a yawn, propped her elbows on the folding table, and studied the quad sheet set out on its surface. The table was slightly too low for her leaning posture to be natural. She stretched her legs out behind her and dug her toes into the rocky ground for support. Her back was tight—to be expected after twenty-two straight days of excavation—and the position, awkward though it was, provided some relief by creating space in the stiff muscles along her spine.

What she really needed was a long hot yoga class. Or a long hot bath. Or maybe a firm massage. Or one full night's sleep. Or all of the above.

But self-care measures would have to wait. The

Rutherford Family Foundation had made it clear to the university that the project was a top priority. And Davina's department head had made it clearer still to her that keeping this major donor happy was Davina's job.

Fast-tracked was the word everyone insisted on using, even though Davina made no secret of her view that *fast-tracking* had no place in archaeological work.

By definition, there were no historical emergencies. What she would find—or not find—under the Jonah Bell Sharecropper Cabin, circa 1865, had been decided over a hundred years ago. There was no legitimate reason to rush to complete the project before the ground froze.

There was *one* reason, she reminded herself: *Money.* It was always about money. Limited funding, expiring grants, and, in this case, a capital campaign by the Rutherford Family Foundation.

The foundation was counting on the discovery of some glitzy, glamorous artifact to splash all over the pleas for donations. This was, in her not-so-humble opinion, a plan that revealed desperation—or delusion. She was excavating a cabin that had been inhabited by a dirt-poor sharecropper, his wife, and their seven children. Whatever her team might manage to unearth, she was confident it would not inspire the denizens of Huntsville's high society to open their gilded pocketbooks and groaning bank vaults.

And so far, at least, she was right. To date, they'd dug up one cracked chamber pot from beneath the collapsed boards of the outdoor privy and a set of dented tin cups in the earth near the house itself. These modest finds were the highlights of the dig. This fact had sent Sully Sullivan (christened Eugene Sullivan, III, but called Sully by everyone except his grandmother) into a fit of red-faced rage that straight-up made Davina giggle because it was so cartoonish.

But there's nothing funny about losing your funding, girl. And Sully, the foundation officer who served as Davina's main contact and prolific writer of checks to the university, had threatened to turn off the money spigot that funded her fieldwork if she didn't find something splashy. And soon.

So here she was, working her tail off to discover something that would appease Margot Rutherford Sullivan's grandson and keep the money flowing.

She sighed and squinted down at the grid. Methodical searching had yielded nothing to appease Sully. She might as well take a different approach.

She closed her eyes, made a circle in the air with her pencil, and jabbed it down on the map at random like a child playing Pin the Tail on the Donkey or a trust fund kid choosing where to travel during her gap year. The graphite tip hit against the table, and she opened her eyes. Her pencil was in square N-12, a spot roughly ninety-two meters from the south wall of the cabin.

Sure, why not?

She tucked her pencil behind her ear, grabbed her shovel, and left the tent, ducking under the white canvas flap, to announce the new location to her assembled team—or, at least, the handful of graduate students who weren't still sleeping off New Year's hangovers and had managed to drag themselves from their warm beds at this ungodly hour.

Five minutes later, she was digging under a gnarled black cherry tree. Seven minutes after that, her shovel struck metal. A frisson of excited surprise shot through her. She had to stop and steady her hands before she shoveled the next load of dirt out of the way.

Thank you, thank you, thank you, she whispered to the heavens.

She called over her shoulder for some help, then kept digging as students streamed toward her from all directions, shouting to one another and waving trowels and brushes. Sheila Mullins, a quiet woman from one of the midwestern states—Ohio, she thought —was the first to reach the spot.

"What've you got, Professor Jones?" Sheila's excitement won out over her shyness as she stepped with exaggerated care over the string that marked the square.

"I'm not sure yet. I hit some metal. Let's hope it's not another tin cup." She was trying to temper her own expectations as much as Sheila's. Possibly more.

Sheila crouched beside her. "I can't imagine how the cups would get all the way out here. We're a good distance from the house."

That meant nothing. Earth shifted over time, buried items migrated from one spot to another. And the Bells had had seven children. If Davina's nieces and nephews were any indication, kids were always wandering off with kitchenware that they later abandoned in random locations.

At the same time, she was sure she'd located something much larger than a cup. *Please let it be a plowshare or a harrow.* But she wasn't in a position to be picky. Large, photogenic farming equipment of any kind would be a godsend.

As she dug, her mind wandered, and she imagined the press conference the Sullivans would no doubt call to announce the discovery. She pictured herself flanked by Sully and his grandmother, explaining the significance of her find. A smile played over her lips.

Sheila's sharp intake of breath dragged her back to the present.

Davina looked down to see a pair of sightless green eyes. They seemed to stare up at her from beneath a veil of dirt.

Her heart thudded in her chest.

"Is ... she's ... dead, right?" Sheila breathed.

Davina swallowed the acerbic response that flew to her lips and nodded. She reached for her soft dusting brush and cleared the earth away with a gentle sweeping motion to reveal the top of an iron coffin. A square glass window set into the coffin displayed a woman's face and part of her hair.

The window was small and dirty, but it was clear that the entombed woman had pale ivory skin. Her hair was pulled back into some sort of knot or bun, but the few tendrils that escaped fell around her face in graceful waves. A high collar that covered most of the corpse's neck was just visible in the bottom of the window. The fabric was filthy, but it was intact, fastened closed with a tarnished brooch.

Davina rocked back on her haunches and caught her lower lip between her teeth. Her blood pounded in her ears. It barely registered when Sheila said her name.

"Professor Jones?"

"Let me think for a minute, Sheila. Please."

She twisted and glanced over her shoulder. The others were still gathering tools and materials. When they finally made their way over to the black cherry tree, their eyes would fall on the most impressive find of Davina Jones' career. Hell, this would be the most impressive find to come out of the entire department in decades—maybe ever.

A genuine Reconstruction-era iron coffin, intact. A shiver zipped up Davina's spine. She almost wanted to pinch herself to prove that this was real life. But her excitement was tempered by doubt.

The well-preserved woman inside, while undeniably dead, couldn't have been dead since the 1800s. Could she?

Davina was no forensic anthropologist, but she was pretty sure that after a hundred and fifty years, give or take, a body would be nothing but bones and goo—if that.

Please, please don't let me be right.

If the woman, for whatever reason, hadn't been dead since the 1800s, that would cast doubt on the coffin's authenticity. Which would bring her work screeching to a halt while experts certified the coffin. She could almost hear Sully blustering about the delay.

She pitched forward to stare into the dead woman's eyes: *Who are you? And what are you doing here?*

2

Huntsville, January 25th, 1870

Darling,

I miss you so. Even as my pen scratches out the words, I hear your sonorous voice forming your response, urging patience, caution, understanding. You are so steadfast, so committed to the cause.

I wish I were as you. But my desires threaten always to burst forth and overwhelm all else. As Mother says, my nature is impetuous, unpredictable, and uncontrollable. I am ruled by my passions. You are ruled by your vision.

Fear not, my darling. I shall follow that which I know you would counsel. Devote myself to the work, our work. The work is so important—the work is all. I know.

And yet.

I long to see you, to touch you, to feel your fingers fumble with my hair clip, releasing my hair, and, with it, me. Your lips covering mine bring hope and light. When I am with you, I am free. Free to be who I am. Free to be yours.

Always yours,
A.

Pittsburgh, PA

The tinkling sound of water flowing over rocks filled Bodhi King's kitchen, the ringtone announcing the arrival of a text. Not just any text—a text from Bette. He put down his teacup and picked up his phone.

Thursday, Jan. 2 • 7:18 AM
BC: Morning. Anything on your calendar this weekend?

He scanned the words and thumbed out a response:

BK: No, all clear. Leigh gets back tomorrow. I can come to you.

They enjoyed a too-infrequent pattern of taking turns visiting one another for long weekends, quick pop-ins, and stolen moments. His schedule was more flexible than hers, so more often than not, he found himself on a bargain airline carrier, flying to Chicago, and then on a bus to Onatah. Bette seemed to find the trip a bit of drudgery, but he viewed it as a chance to hone his mindful attention.

The winter holidays had presented a challenge, though. As the only single, childless law enforcement officer in the department, Onatah Police Chief Bette Clark made it a habit to cover the Thanksgiving weekend shifts singlehandedly so her men and women could spend the time with their families. Then, she always spent five days at her sister's place in the Pacific Northwest between Christmas and New Year's. For his part, Bodhi had committed to housesit —and birdsit, Eliza Doolittle, the macaw, squawked a reminder—for his tenant for most of December.

The result? Six long, cold weeks of separation.

He retrieved his mug and sipped his morning tea as the little dots on his phone blinked to let him know Bette was typing.

BC: Better idea: there's a conference of small-town police chiefs at some chichi resort in Alabama Fri-Mon. Town budget has a surplus. Will pay for my plus-one. I know it's short notice but wanna meet me there?

He frowned down at the screen. A fancy resort in Alabama didn't exactly scream 'Bodhi and Bette.' They were more of a 'tent in a state park' couple. And the thought of the citizens of Onatah paying for his boon-doggle sent a squiggle of discomfort through his gut. He focused on the sensation in his stomach and considered his response.

BK: I need to think about it.

BC: What's to think about? It's a getaway. With me. ;-)

BK: The allure isn't lost on me.

BC: But?

BK: But I don't want to freeload.

BC: It's not freeloading. Mayor D insisted I invite you.

He reached for the phone to compose a response, but the dots were blinking again. He waited.

BC: Grr. Fine, think it over. I have to run anyway.

BK: May your day be peaceful and safe.

BC: You could just say bye like a normal person.

BK: I could.
But you know you love it.

BC: Matter of fact, I do. Really gotta go. Talk later?

BK: OK.

BC: We need to book your ticket today if you're coming.

He had no response to that, so he silenced his phone, returned it to the table, picked up his mug, and headed into the quiet living room. Unlike Bette, he had no pressing appointments. He could take some time to sit in meditation with his reaction to her invitation. With luck, he'd gain a better understanding of his hesitation.

He finished his tea, then lowered himself to the sun-streaked hardwood floor and reached for his worn, well-used meditation cushion. Eliza Doolittle peered around the corner, twisting her head at an angle to peer at him through the wire bars of her cage with one bright, black eye.

"Namaste, Bodhi. Namaste."

He smiled at the bird. "Namaste, Eliza Doolittle."

She withdrew her head and preened her feathers. He arranged his sit bones on the cushion and closed his eyes.

He focused first on his breath—*in, out, in, out*—and found his center. He zipped through a body scan, checking in lightly with each part of his body. His tension was in the twist of his gut and in the sudden tightness of his chest, his heart, really.

He addressed each in turn. His stomach was jumpy, uneasy. The feeling had grabbed hold of his belly during the text exchange with Bette. Specifically, when she'd explained that Onatah would pay for him to accompany her to the conference.

Was he having some macho reaction to his girl-friend paying his way—at least in a manner of speaking? He didn't think it likely, but he held the idea in his mind for a long moment, considered it from all angles, then swiped it away. No. That wasn't the source of his discomfort.

What then?

His mind was a blank. Quiet. No snippets of conversation, no images, no hints whirled through his consciousness to suggest what the problem might be.

He abandoned the effort and turned to a *metta bhavana* meditation, sending out good thoughts and warm wishes in turn to his loved ones, his friends, his rivals, and, finally, his enemies. The loving-kindness exercise softened his heart and relaxed his belly. So he continued to sit.

He sat and listened to the soft thud of his heart, the distant tick of a clock, the faint whistle of the wind through the bare trees outside.

He sat long past the time that his tea cooled in its mug.

He sat until Eliza Doolittle cawed, *"Bodhi's sleeping. Shh."*

He opened his eyes and twisted to look over his shoulder at the bird. "Not sleeping, Eliza Doolittle."

She nodded, eager and excited. *"Good. Time to feed the bird."*

He rose and headed to the kitchen. She was, after all, right about that.

She eagerly pecked at the handful of berries and nuts he offered. When she finished, he gave her fresh water then stroked her brilliant blue crown.

"Leigh is coming home," he told her.

She trilled, a contented sound from deep within her throat.

3

Davina peered down into the woman's sightless jade eyes as if they might hold answers instead of endless questions.

In the pocket of her lab coat, her watch beeped. Game time. Any minute, Sully Sullivan and his formidable grandmother, Margot Rutherford Sullivan, the matriarch of the family, CEO of ... well, everything related to the Rutherford fortune, and the most influential person in town, would arrive to view the coffin.

A knock sounded on the windowless laboratory door. Davina raked her fingers through her hair and buttoned her white coat as it if were armor. Then she strode across the room and pulled open the door.

Margot stepped through it like a queen, regal and straight-backed. Davina could easily imagine a crown atop the perfectly coiffed strawberry blonde curls, no doubt fresh from her weekly wash and blow out. Her pale blue eyes were lively and alert, and her thin frame was weighed down with jewelry. Dazzling rings dripped from every finger. Heavy earrings hung from her lobes, sparkling in the weak sun that streamed through the low basement windows. A chunky string of pearls encircled her throat. She looked like a million bucks, literally.

Margot curved her mouth into a smile, but Davina wasn't fooled. She'd seen the steel that girded this particular magnolia. Her southern lady demeanor was largely camouflage. Or, to be accurate, aggressive mimicry. To Davina's mind, the matriarch of the Rutherford family was no different than an alligator snapping turtle.

Jace, her youngest nephew, had shown her one of the turtles last summer at the river. The thing looked more like a dinosaur than a turtle, with its scaly skin and spiky shell. They'd squatted in the long grass and watched the creature as it lay motionless in the still water. Jace told her to focus on the turtle's open mouth, where a bubble-gum pink appendage hung from the tip of its tongue. The turtle wiggled the pink thing, making it squirm and dance just like a worm. As soon as it lured in an unsuspecting minnow, it snapped its powerful jaws shut.

Margot Rutherford Sullivan was an alligator snapping turtle, and her Southern belle exterior was nothing more than a fake worm. Davina would do well to remember that. She'd hate to end up as turtle chow.

Margot's grandson trotted in on her heel. As always, when Margot was in the room, Davina hardly noticed Sully. For all his blather the rest of the time, he was virtually mute around Margot.

"Mrs. Rutherford, Mr. Sullivan, I'm so excited for you to see this."

"That's clear. I can't recall the last time I received a telephone call before nine o'clock in the morning."

Snap went the turtle.

"I apologize if I woke you—either of you. But a discovery like this, honestly, it's worth getting out of bed for."

Margot waved away the apology with one heavily be-ringed hand. "By all means, then, show us what you found, Professor Jones."

She guided them to the table that held the coffin. "Earlier this morning, we started to dig in a new location. We located this Reconstruction-Era iron coffin."

"Why?" Sully asked.

"Why what?"

"Why did you deviate from your plan. I thought you were focusing on the areas that had the strongest hits on that remote sensing device you showed me?"

Talk about missing the point. She was about to show them an astonishing find, and he wanted to know why she hadn't followed her predetermined procedure.

"Divine inspiration, I guess."

Margot arched a brow. "Really?"

"Well, maybe equal parts inspiration and desperation. Sully ... er, Mr. Sullivan has explained that it's crucial to find something dazzling to serve as the centerpiece for your fundraising efforts." She swept her arms out and gestured to the coffin like a game show host. "This is it!"

They leaned forward and craned their necks to peer down at it.

"And you say it's iron?" Margot's nostrils flared as if the metal was somehow distasteful.

"Yes. Airtight iron coffins were popular in the U.S. from the 1840s until about the 1870s—pre-Civil War through Reconstruction. The original iron coffin was invented by a man named Almond Fisk. Based on the quick research I did this morning using the university's online collections, this one dates to the 1860s or 70s."

"How can you tell?"

"By the shape. The original design was effective, but it closely resembled a sarcophagus. It never really caught on with the public, because people thought it was creepy. Mr. Fisk eventually licensed the idea to a handful of other manufacturers, who later introduced plainer designs, like this one."

"I see." Margot's tone was flat.

Davina's gut twisted. Why weren't they more enthusiastic about her discovery? Did they not understand how extraordinary it was?

Just push through. Make them feel it.

"And it's difficult to see through the glass, but the woman in the coffin is remarkably well-preserved. Once we've cleaned the coffin, I think the public will be lining up to view her. With luck, we should be able to see the detail in her brooch and—"

"Brooch?" A flicker of interest crossed Margot's face.

Ah, right. Look at her. Of course, she's interested in the jewelry. Run with it.

"Here, come closer so you can see it better." She touched Margot's elbow and positioned her at the head of the coffin so she would have a clear angle. "See the pin at her throat?"

Margot made a small noise, like a breath catching

in her throat, and stared for a long moment as if she were spellbound.

Got her.

"Grandmother?"

Sully's prompting broke the spell. Margot blinked and turned to her grandson. For a wild second, Davina thought she saw a warning in the woman's eye. But then it was gone.

"It's difficult to believe that woman has been dead since the mid-1800s. Impossible, actually."

Davina tried not to hear the ominous emphasis Margot placed on *impossible.* But it was, well, impossible not to. She caught her lower lip between her teeth and thought for a moment.

When she spoke, she chose her words with care. "I can authenticate the coffin. I have the requisite expertise. I can't date a corpse, that would take a forensic specialist. But it stands to reason—"

"We can't guess, Davina." Margot's voice was kind but firm. Very, very firm.

"It's not a guess. It's logic. And I think you may not realize what a crowning achievement this is. This is *it.* The big, splashy find that Sully wants for his capital campaign? You have it. You can sell tickets to a special exhibit. You'll get international interest. This is huge."

"It is huge," Sully agreed.

Another look from his grandmother. *Snap* goes the turtle.

He clamped his mouth shut.

"It *could be,*" Margot agreed. "But we have to be careful, measured. I understand that this is your big break, dear. But surely *you* understand that we have to proceed deliberately and cautiously."

Davina's moment was slipping out of her grasp. She was being set adrift. Her legs threatened to buckle.

"What are you saying?"

Margot gave Sully a small nod. *Go ahead.*

"We're saying we need to be absolutely sure before we make an announcement that both the coffin and the woman are from the Reconstruction Era."

"You're going to sit on it?" Her mouth hung open. She knew, but she didn't care.

"We're going to be patient. And we're going to ask you to do the same. We'll reach out to the forensic anthropologists, forensic archaeologists, what have you. We'll assess and confirm. And then we'll share the news, assuming your beliefs can be verified," Margot explained.

Davina's temper was rising. She could feel it. So she clamped her mouth shut and nodded.

Margot took a final look at the woman. "The brooch ... extraordinary," she murmured.

"I have a necklace just like it," Davina offered, hoping to smooth over the unpleasantness.

Margot's eyes traced Davina's face. She laughed lightly. "Not like this brooch, you don't."

4

Bodhi was washing his hands when a car pulled into the driveway. He squinted at the vehicle while he dried his hands on a checked dishtowel. He couldn't place the powder blue minivan.

Who would be visiting him so early in the morning? He'd been awake for hours, but it was hardly a civilized time for a pop-in.

The driver emerged, clutching a bakery bag, and Bodhi smiled when he recognized Saul David's distinctive loping gait. He hurried to the kitchen door to greet his former co-worker.

"Saul, this is a surprise," he said as he pulled open the door.

Saul hurried inside and thrust the bag toward

Bodhi. "Pastries from that vegan bakery you like. You got any coffee?"

He stamped the snow off his boots, then shrugged out of his heavy wool overcoat.

"Thanks, and I do. I'll put on a pot in a minute. Here, give me your coat." He placed the breakfast goodies on the counter and reached for the coat and the long plaid scarf that Saul unwound from his neck.

"It's frigid out there." He blew into his bare hands to warm them.

"No gloves?"

Saul jerked a thumb over his shoulder toward the driveway. "My car's in the shop, so I had to borrow Mona's mom-mobile. I'm sure they're in there somewhere, buried under a mound of schoolbooks, gym clothes, and half-eaten lunches."

He shuddered, and Bodhi figured it was due more to the state of the family minivan than the chill in the air.

"Well, we'll get you warmed up with a mug of hot coffee."

"Now you're talking."

Saul pulled out a kitchen chair and flopped into it while Bodhi measured out the coffee and water.

"*Hello, Saul David,*" the bird chirped from her perch.

"Hi, Eliza Doolittle."

Once the machine was percolating and the coffee was underway, Bodhi joined his guest at the table and offered him first choice of the baked goods.

Saul waved the box away. "Nah, I already ate. Those are for you."

Bodhi eyed him. "You need a favor."

"Actually, you're wrong for once. I have no bizarre, unexplainable deaths to explain. All the bodies in the morgue right now have run-of-the-mill causes of death. Heart attacks from shoveling snow, head-on collisions on icy roads, and fire victims from malfunctioning electric blankets and heaters. 'Tis the season." There was a hint of disappointment in the medical examiner's voice at not having any exotic deaths to offer.

"So, you borrowed your wife's car, ventured out in bad weather, stopped at a bakery you don't care for, all during your vacation week, to show up unannounced because ..."

Saul nodded toward the carafe. "Coffee's done."

Bodhi crossed the kitchen and pulled two mugs down from the cabinet. Saul was stalling. Which was not like him. Chief Medical Examiner David was known for his forthright manner. He didn't pull his punches.

Bodhi's chest sank, suddenly heavy. He returned to the table and passed Saul a mug of coffee.

"I don't want to come work for you," he said in a neutral voice.

Saul's laugh rumbled up, deep and hearty. "While you have a standing offer, I'm not holding my breath on that front. No, this visit isn't about forensic pathology at all. It's ... personal."

"Are you and Mona having problems?"

Saul swigged the coffee before answering. "Not my personal life. Yours."

"Mine?" Bodhi cocked his head. "What about my personal life?"

"More like, *what* personal life, don't you mean?" Saul arched an eyebrow at him.

"Pardon?" He tore off a corner from a cranberry scone and nibbled it while he awaited clarification.

"You've been dating this lady police chief for, what, two years now?"

"About."

"Mona and I haven't met her. Maisy hasn't met her. Sasha and Leo haven't met her. As far as I can tell, nobody's met her."

"She lives in Onatah, Saul. It's not as if we can get together for happy hour with the gang at a moment's notice."

"Idaho isn't on the moon, buddy."

"She lives in Illinois, Saul. Still Illinois. Not Idaho, not Indiana, not Iowa."

Saul snaked out a hand and cadged a chocolate cruller. "The midwestern states should have picked another letter if they wanted people to tell them apart. Who decided they all needed to start with 'I'?"

Bodhi raised his hands in an unconcerned gesture. "I wasn't consulted."

"No matter. We're straying from the point."

"Which is?" He was genuinely curious. Saul's point, or aim, or whatever he was hoping to achieve, was a mystery.

"Which is that you keep Bette at a distance. Why? You seem happy with her. Embrace your relationship. Move to Onatah already. Nothing's keeping you here. You can be a forensic consultant from anywhere. *Commit* already, man."

Bodhi blinked at the fierce note in Saul's voice. "Where is this coming from? Is Mona behind this?"

Saul dismissed the question with a shake of his head. "We've talked about it, sure. But, no. This is coming from my heart."

Bodhi hid his surprise behind his mug and waited for Saul to elaborate. For a long moment, the only sound in the kitchen was the hiss of the radiator near the door, releasing hot steamy air. Saul looked down at his hands and nodded several times as if he was pumping himself up.

Finally, he raised his head and continued, "If you love Bette, you need to take a leap of faith, take a risk. Life is short. Sharing it with someone makes it enjoyable."

"You don't understand. The Buddha counsels us to practice non-attachment."

"Yeah, yeah. And monks are celibate. I know. But regular Buddhists, they get married, have kids, whatever. Right?"

"Some. Not all."

"Not you, you mean."

"Saul, I'm happy with the path I chose."

Saul locked eyes with him and fixed him with a piercing gaze. "Are you? Or are you afraid you'll hurt this woman the way you hurt Eliza?"

Shock rushed through his veins like a spray of ice water at the sound of Eliza's name in Saul's mouth. Before he could formulate a response, the macaw shrieked.

"Bodhi hurt Eliza? Bodhi hurt Eliza. Oooh, no, poor Eliza Doolittle." Her already shrill voice wavered and increased in pitch.

Saul closed his eyes and shook his head. Bodhi

lifted the bird off her perch and soothed her.

"Shh, pretty bird. Not you; a different Eliza. But nobody's been hurt. It's okay."

He smoothed her ruffled feathers, figuratively and literally. After a moment, she hopped from his arm to his shoulder and settled into a comfortable position.

He eyed his friend. "I'm not sure what you're getting at."

Saul went on, "You say you're following a path of enlightenment, and I respect that. But you can take that path and make room in your life for connection, true connection, with another person. I don't think it's Buddhism that's stopping you—I think it's your history with ... uh, Dr. Rollins." He cut his eyes toward the regal blue and gold bird on Bodhi's shoulder.

Eliza Doolittle tilted her head and blinked at the coroner, unperturbed.

Bodhi, in contrast, was not. His emotions roiled, churning and seething. The memory of Eliza Rollins, and the way he'd treated her so long ago, still held sway over him.

He slowed and centered his breath, then chose his words with care. "I appreciate your concern. You're a good man and a good friend. But you're just wrong about this. You don't know what happened between us. It was a long time ago ... and I was a different person."

Saul held up a hand.

"Please, if anyone understands the concept, it's me. As your friend, I'm not inclined to judge you harshly. As a Jew and as a sinner, I'm in no position to judge you at all. But I suspect *you* are judging yourself and that's why you keep Bette at a distance."

"I don't keep her at a distance."

Saul twisted his mouth in a display of skepticism.

"I don't," Bodhi insisted. "Besides, I made things right when I saw Eliza in Canada the year before last." *Or, as I right as I could, at any rate.*

Saul raised his palms. "Fine. I've said my piece. Just think about it, huh? You deserve more than a tenuous long-distance arrangement—and the mysterious Chief Clark no doubt does as well."

"For your information, we're taking a weekend trip together. Tomorrow. Is that serious enough for you?"

Saul grinned. "A getaway? That's great. Where to?"

"Alabama. Some fancy resort."

Saul clapped him on the back. "Why didn't you say so? Need a lift to the airport?"

"That'd be great. I ... need to confirm my flight time. I'll text you the details."

"Sure, sure." Saul drained his coffee mug and

pushed back his chair. "I should get back. A week off school in this weather means our kids are climbing the walls. I'm sure Mona could use a hand."

"Thanks for the treats. And the conversation."

"I hope I haven't overstepped."

Bodhi walked with him to the door. "Not at all. I'm glad you brought it up. It clarified some things for me."

Saul flashed him a quizzical look but didn't ask.

Bodhi showed him out, closed the door, and picked up his phone.

BK: I'm in.

BC: Really? Great! I didn't even have to play my ace card.

BK: ???

BC: The resort has a meditation garden and miles and miles of mountain hiking trails.

BK: Perfect. Can't wait.

5

Rutherford Nature Preserve and Open-Air Museum
Friday afternoon

Davina checked her reflection in the mirror hanging over her lab sink. The purpose behind a mirror at a sink meant for washing hands and sterilizing equipment was a mystery to her. But there was no reason to let that stop her from using it to her advantage, she thought as she pulled out her teddy bear brown lipstick and lined her lips.

She'd almost opted for red, but she needed to

come across as a responsible professional. Hence the brown lipstick, the hair coaxed into submission, and the fresh, crisp white lab coat she'd run home to fetch. And the ornate necklace. Although, if she were being honest, she was wearing the pendant mainly to shove it in Margot Rutherford Sullivan's face.

After one last mirror check and a final glance at the coffin, she strode purposefully toward the door. She took care to lock the lab behind her before she headed for the worn marble stairs that led from the basement to the main floor.

Oh, and don't forget the sensible heels in place of her mud-covered boots. They clicked and clacked against the marble as she hurried up to the wide front hall and careened across the gleaming lobby. She paused just inside the entrance to catch her breath.

She stood there for a good five minutes. Her nerves settled into anticipation, then boredom, and, finally, irritation when she realized she was being stood up. She was pulling her phone out to check if the local culture reporter had left a message when Marvin Washington, the museum's chief security officer, rounded the corner and beelined toward her.

"Afternoon, Professor Jones."

"Hi, Officer Washington."

They were on a first-name basis. After all, she'd grown up around the corner from his uncle's people. But here, in the museum, as the only two black professionals, they kept it formal.

"I suppose you're waiting for that reporter from WLAL?"

The note of resignation in his voice made her pause, but, after a moment, she nodded. "Yes. Did she call? Is her crew running late?"

Maybe there'd been an accident and they were stuck in traffic. Or maybe there's been an accident and they were covering it. Or maybe—

"No, I'm afraid not. But Mrs. Rutherford Sullivan and Mr. Sullivan want to see you. They asked me to send you up to the boardroom."

Oh.

"Oh. Well, that's going to be awkward. Lisette Chase from WLAL is coming out to interview me about the coffin I found this morning. I promised her an exclusive. And she'll be here any minute." She made a show of checking the time on her watch.

"I'm afraid she won't, Professor."

"Of course she will...." The expression on Marvin's face stopped her cold. "What happened?"

"Mrs. Rutherford Sullivan called Lisette up herself

when she heard about the interview. She said the interview is canceled and said you aren't authorized to speak on behalf of the foundation regarding the Bell dig site or any artifacts found there."

Fire roared in Davina's belly. Her hands tightened into fists without her realizing. She shook her head. "She didn't. She wouldn't."

The inside corners of Marvin's thick eyebrows turned up while the outside corners of his lips drooped down. He looked unspeakably sad.

"She did. I'm sorry, Dav—professor. I know that coffin is a big deal in your field."

She couldn't think of a single word to say. Not even a syllable or noise of acknowledgment. She swallowed, then stumbled into the elevator lobby, fear warring with rage inside her.

Fear won out. When she raised her fist to knock on the door, her hand shook. She lifted and lowered her shoulders, shook out her trembling hands, and inhaled and exhaled several deep, slow breaths before rapping her knuckles against the door.

"Yes?" Sully called as if he weren't expecting her.

"It's me." The words came out in a broken croak. She cleared her throat and tried again, pitching her voice lower. "It's Davina."

"Enter."

She arched a brow at the order but pushed open the door. She crossed the threshold and stood in front of the twelve-foot-long mahogany table. Its surface was so highly polished that her drawn, anxious face stared up at her. She relaxed the muscles in her forehead and watched her reflected brow unwrinkle.

Sully sat in one of the massive claw-footed leather chairs, a porcelain cup of tea at his elbow, staring down at a tablet. From just inside the doorway, she couldn't see what he was reading. Financial statements, if she had to guess.

He glanced up at her over the top of his reading glasses. "What's a nine-letter word for 'lacking essentials, such as food and shelter'? Starts with a 'p.'"

P words, none of which Sully had so much as a passing acquaintance with, ran through her mind: *penniless, poverty-ridden, penurious*—that had nine letters.

"Oh, and it ends with an 'n.' Maybe." He removed his glasses and twirled them by one titanium stem while he blinked up at her, waiting for her to provide an answer.

"Try 'privation.'" She bit back a laugh at the notion of Sully or any of his crowd trying privation on for size.

He returned the glasses to his face and tapped his

stylus against the screen. "That works." He gave a satisfied nod, then powered off his digital crossword puzzle and set the device on the table next to his teacup.

She waited for him to thank her, but he just looked at her with a raised eyebrow and an expression of the mildest interest.

She cleared her throat. "Is, um, Mrs. Rutherford joining us?"

He gave an airy wave toward the hallway. "Grandmother will be along eventually. Punctuality isn't her strong suit."

Of course not. Another 'p' word more suited for the plebeian class than the posh. The bitter thought popped, unbidden, into her mind, but she kept her face neutral, an expressionless mask she'd perfected while defending her thesis back in the day. She clasped her hands together behind her back and waited.

Sully poured himself a cup of tea and fussed with the silver tongs until he managed to fish a sugar cube out of a bowl that she placed as a mid-nineteenth century piece.

A hidden panel in the silk-covered wall behind Sully's chair slid open to reveal Margot. Talk about making an entrance.

Margot fluttered her eyelashes at her grandson, who belatedly leaped to his feet and yanked out a chair for her. Once seated, she gestured with one heavily be-ringed hand for Davina to take a seat as well.

"Professor Jones, don't you look nice all dressed up. Pour the child a cup of tea, Eugene."

While Sully attended to the tea and passed it to Davina, Margot got right down to business. "Going behind our backs and reaching out to the media? Unacceptable, of course. We're suspending your access to the dig site and the museum."

Luckily, Davina had just lifted the dainty porcelain cup to her mouth when Margot made her proclamation. She was pretty sure she'd have sputtered tea all over the expensive table if she'd had a mouthful. As it was, her hand shook as she lowered the cup, which clattered against the saucer.

"Surely that's not necessary."

"You disregarded a clear directive, Professor," Eugene pointed out.

Davina shook her head, and her words rushed out, tripping over one another in her desperation. "I didn't mean to offend you. I wasn't going to opine as to the age of the corpse. It's just . . . such a significant find."

Margot narrowed her eyes. "Yes. And as we

explained to you just hours ago, it will be announced in due course after the proper procedures have been followed."

"Respectfully, I think you're making a mistake."

Sully leaned back and widened his eyes, surprised and maybe a smidge impressed at her spunk. His grandmother, however, was decidedly unimpressed. She pressed her lips together in a flat line and stared, steely-eyed, at Davina for a long, silent moment.

She forced herself not to fidget under the woman's gaze.

Finally, Margot snapped, "I didn't ask for your thoughts, Professor Jones. But, now, I'll share mine. I think it's curious that you're in such a rush to claim your credit. It's as if you want to make an impression before your story falls apart and you're revealed to be a fraud."

"I beg your pardon?" She tried to match the older woman's frosty, formal tone.

She reached for her teacup then thought better of it. Adrenaline and anxiety still coursed through her body. She wasn't sure her hands would be steady. So, she placed them palms-down on the table and waited.

Sully cleared his throat, but Margot responded before he had the chance to speak.

"If you must know, Lewis Dexter came out to see the corpse."

"Why?"

"My dear girl, you found a dead body. The chief of police has an interest—and a theory of culpability."

"A theory of what?" She winced at how squeaky her voice sounded, then coughed and went on at a lower pitch, "Does Chief Dexter think someone on *my* team committed a crime?"

"No, dear. He thinks *you* may have." Margot flashed a knife's-edge smile over her teacup.

Davina's brain froze. It simply stopped working for several seconds. Then it kicked into overdrive, and her thoughts raced so fast she couldn't keep up.

"What am I being accused of, exactly?" She managed to keep her tone level and calm, but she couldn't still her fingers, which raked through her short-shorn curls as she struggled to understand.

"The working theory, as I understand it, is that you were under pressure to find something impressive. And when all you turned up were some old cups and a cracked chamberpot, you improvised."

"And, by improvised, you mean ... I buried a counterfeit iron coffin?" She turned her head from Margot to Sully, blinking slowly. "You realize that's nonsensical, right? That would be archaeological fraud."

"Not to mention tampering with a corpse and who knows how many other crimes," Sully noted.

Her face heated. "That, too."

Margot took over in her calm ladylike way, "We have no doubt you will clear your name with the authorities and, equally important, the scientific community. But, until the coffin and its occupant are both examined and authenticated, we simply cannot acknowledge that you are affiliated with the Rutherford Family Foundation—or the museum. So, you are suspended until this is resolved. Appearances, you understand."

She didn't understand. Not at all.

"How long?"

"As long as it takes."

"What about the dig?"

"Suspended indefinitely," Sully told her.

He gestured for her identification badge, and she responded automatically. Her fingers moved to the clasp, unclipped the plastic badge holder, and deposited it in his outstretched hand.

Margot was staring at her with laser focus. She shrank under the scrutiny and reached for her necklace, rubbing the filigree pattern with her thumb in an absent, self-soothing gesture.

She felt someone standing behind her. When she turned, dazed, and saw Marvin looming in the doorway, she stood and stumbled out of the room. She followed him numbly down to the lab to gather her personal belongings and then out of the building.

6

Bodhi checked into the stone-and-timber Lodge on the Mountain several hours before Bette's plane landed. He asked for directions to the Japanese Garden, dumped his bag in his room, then hiked the Rainbow Loop Trail to the meditation garden.

He reached the red *torii* gate, stepped under the arch, and followed the groomed pebble path through a stand of towering bamboo. A short walk later, the bamboos were replaced by fiery red maple trees and short, squat hosta bushes. The path looped around to a scarlet-lacquered footbridge.

He crossed the bridge and followed the path to a building styled like a Japanese teahouse. Solid cedar construction, a red-painted, paneless, circular window, and an inlaid floor made up the open-air structure.

He explored the small building, then took the well-tended and raked spiraling path that led out into the garden's cherry trees, the pond with lotus leaves floating on the surface, and the Alabama woods beyond. He turned his focus away from the tranquil landscape and toward his feet touching the ground. He chose a small circle within the concentric path and began his meditation.

Walking meditation always cleared his mind; more than that, it crystallized his thoughts. He clasped his hands behind his back and slowed his pace.

He raised his right foot and moved it forward.

I lift my right foot. My foot greets the air.

He placed it on the path.

I lower my right foot. My foot caresses the earth.

He raised his left foot and stepped forward.

I lift my left foot. My foot greets the air.

He returned his foot to the path.

I lower my left foot. My foot caresses the earth.

He lowered his eyelids until they were half-closed. Then he continued along the circle taking measured steps and using exaggerated motions. As he stepped, the hum of disquiet that had been buzzing in his ear all day faded, then dissipated.

After he'd accepted Bette's invitation, he worried whether he'd done so just to prove Saul wrong. He hoped not. That would violate his vow to engage in right action, as it skirted the edges of sexual misconduct by misleading Bette. But as he circled through the garden, his concern fell away.

He enjoyed Bette's company. He treated her with care and respect. He honored her. The time spent with her was a blessing to him. There was no reason to attach negative intent to it.

He opened his eyes, exhaled, and keyed back in on his surroundings. He filled his lungs with the crisp winter air. Dry fallen leaves crunched and crackled under his feet as he took one slow and considered step after another.

He was halfway back to the teahouse structure when he spotted a tawny deer peering out from behind a tall, ferny bush. The doe was thin and sleek and small. And curious and unafraid of him.

He sank soundlessly to the ground and folded himself into the lotus position while the doe watched with liquid chocolate eyes. After he settled onto the gravel path, he extended his left hand toward the still, watchful animal, turning his palm skyward. She didn't hesitate. She pranced out of the brush, crunching the gravel under her hooves.

In a heartbeat, she was nuzzling his empty palm. Her nose was damp and warm against his skin. He reached out with his right hand and stroked the white spot on her forehead, an irregular star-shaped patch. They looked into one another's eyes.

A sudden, loud *thwack* echoed through the woods. The doe bolted, kicking up dried leaves with her hooves as she fled away from the sound. She melted away into the trees, and Bodhi tilted his head to place the noise that had startled her.

After a moment, it came again: A sharp, cracking noise—not a gunshot, not a mechanical thing. It sounded almost as if someone were chopping wood. But the rhythm was wrong. Too slow, too irregular.

He stepped off the groomed path and into the woods. The fleeting question of whether the northern Alabama mountains were home to bears flitted through his consciousness. He pushed it aside and continued to creep toward the noise.

He spotted the source in a clearing about ten yards away. A tall, muscular black woman with cropped, natural hair was throwing an ax into a large pine tree stump. She stood roughly twenty feet from the stump. She squared her feet to line herself up with her target, squinted, and then took a step forward. As she stepped, she swung the ax down past her thigh then raised it over her shoulder in a quick motion. She brought her arm forward and released the ax. It arced and whizzed through the air, straight for the stump. It cleaved the wood with a crack and stuck. Before the air had stilled, she jogged forward to yank the ax out. Then she returned to her spot to do it again.

Bodhi watched, shielded from her view by a row of fir trees. Through the branches, he could see that sweat dotted her brow and her step began to slow with each ax retrieval, but she showed no signs of stopping.

Heave, thwack, retrieve. Heave, thwack, retrieve.

Throwing the ax seemed to hold a meditative quality for the woman, not unlike his recent walk through the garden.

He pushed up his sleeve to check his watch. Bette's plane would be landing any minute. Time to turn back.

As he stepped back from the copse of trees, a large twig cracked underfoot. The sound echoed through the woods. He froze and craned his neck over his shoulder. Sure enough, the noise had caught the attention of the ax thrower, who wheeled in his direction, gripping the weapon two-handed.

"Who's there?"

Her tone was filled not with fear, but with anger. Of course, she was armed, so it was no surprise that she wasn't scared. He'd once seen the victim of an ax murderer when he was working for the Allegheny County Medical Examiner's Office. *Gruesome* didn't do the sight justice.

He quickly stepped off from behind the fir trees with his arms raised, his palms near his head. "I didn't mean to scare you."

He took two paces toward her. She jabbed the ax in the air. "Stay where you are."

He complied.

"Why are you creeping around in the woods?"

"I'm staying at the resort back there. I was walking in the Japanese garden, and the sound of your ax throwing caught my attention. I came over to investigate the noise." He inclined his head in the direction from which he'd come.

"Well, now you know what the noise was." She held the ax awkwardly in front of her.

"I do. So I'll be on my way."

They stared at each other for a long moment. Something in her tense expression made him add, "Again, I apologize for startling you. Have a peaceful day."

As he turned to leave, she barked out a short mirthless laugh. "That's unlikely."

"Pardon?"

"I'm unlikely to have a peaceful day seeing as how my professional life is falling apart."

Bodhi absorbed this news, then he nodded. "Is there anything I can do to help?"

"Not unless you happen to be able to determine the time and manner of a death," she snorted.

His full-throated laughter sent her eyebrows shooting up her forehead. "There's something funny about that?"

"Yes, there is. As it happens, I *can* determine the time and manner of death."

"Get the heck out of here." She waved the ax in annoyance.

"It's true. I'm a forensic pathologist. My name is Bodhi King. I used to work as a medical examiner in Pittsburgh, but now I'm a consultant."

She gaped at him. After a long moment she found her voice. "You're a forensic pathology consultant?"

"Yes, ma'am. I consult on unusual or puzzling cases."

She shook her head, disbelief warring with hope in her eyes. "Oh, this is an unusual case, all right. But why ... I mean ... how do you happen to be wandering around the Alabama woods just when I need your expertise?"

He studied her face while he formed his response.

"I could say it's because my romantic partner is the police chief of a town in Illinois and she's here this weekend for a conference of small-town police chiefs, so I tagged along as her guest. That would be the truth. But it's also true that, in my experience, the universe often provides what we need when we need it. So it's equally valid to say I'm here because you need me to be."

"What, like God will provide?"

"Something along those lines."

"So, you believe in miracles?"

"In a manner of speaking. I think we can bring about our own miracles if we're attentive and enlightened."

"Enlightened," she echoed wonderingly. "You a Buddhist or something?"

"Yes."

"Hmm, well, I don't know about enlightenment, but if you really can help me then I say you're an angel in disguise. Can you help me?" Her voice faltered, and she lowered her hand so that the ax rested near her thigh.

"I can certainly try."

"I'd appreciate that—very much." She switched the ax to her left hand and stuck out her right. "I'm Davina Truth Jones. I'm a professor in the archaeology department at the university down in Huntsville."

Bodhi shook her proffered hand. Her skin was cool and rough. Calluses covered her fingers and a bandage covered what he suspected was a blister on her palm. She had working hands. Hands that dug into the unyielding earth to pry out its secrets.

"I'm glad to meet you, Professor Jones."

"Please, Davina's fine, Doctor King."

"Then you should call me Bodhi."

She smiled faintly. "Okay, Bodhi. So, now what?"

"Tell me about the body." His practice was not to call people bodies, corpses, or the deceased when he knew their names. Death strips us of our dignity in both small and large ways. There was no reason to let it strip us of our humanity. But, in this case, he didn't have a name . . . yet.

"For the past several months, I've been running an excavation at the Rutherford Open-Air Museum and Preserve. The dig site is the farm and cabin of a black sharecropper named Jonah Bell. Mr. Bell died in 1885, his wife, also black, followed in 1888. Yesterday, we uncovered an iron coffin buried under a black cherry tree not far from where their house sat. There was a body inside."

"Not Mr. or Mrs. Bell, I take it?"

"Right. It's a well-preserved female, white. Also, records show the Bells and their children were all buried in the Free Baptist churchyard."

"And the woman in the coffin, you have no idea who she is?"

"None. Apparently, our police chief, Chief Dexter, has this wild-eyed theory that I somehow found an empty iron coffin lying around somewhere and stuffed a body into it so I could find it. It's sheer idiocy. But it's gotten me suspended from the dig, and it's put the dig itself on hold."

"You're a person of interest in a police investigation?"

Her eyes narrowed at the question, but, after a moment, she answered, "I guess so. I don't know for sure. An officer took my statement after we found the body. We had to call, you know, as a formality. But nobody interrogated me or anything. The guy who came out seemed bored by it all."

"So why would they suspend you?"

A bitter laugh. "Optics. Appearances. And I did call a press conference without permission. But, c'mon. This coffin is a huge discovery. I just hope they don't give the university any ideas."

"About the unidentified dead woman—have there

been any recent disappearances? I mean, is someone missing who fits her description?"

"No, not that I know of." She paused and drew a deep breath, "Look, I know it sounds wild, but like I told you, that iron coffin was made for her . . . in the mid-1800s."

"You may well be right. It's certainly possible. But to confirm it, we probably really need a forensic anthropologist."

"So, you can't help me?" Her lower lip wobbled, and she bit down on it, hard.

"Well, I've read about iron coffins in some journals. To date, only a handful have been excavated and examined. Some of them were breached over time, water or air got in and ... you can imagine the condition of the body. But, in a handful of cases, when the coffins were airtight and the bodies had been embalmed, they were mistaken for contemporary corpses. I could make a preliminary assessment, and I could certainly hazard a guess as to cause of death. But to accurately date a corpse that old, a forensic anthropologist would come in handy."

She shifted her ax from one hand to the other as she processed the new information. "Embalming wasn't that common back then. At least, not in the U.S."

"That's true. But it wasn't unheard of, and it was becoming more commonplace—especially among the well-off."

"Anyone whose family could afford an iron coffin was affluent enough to afford embalming," she agreed.

"So, our working theory is that a rich, white woman from the post-Civil War era was embalmed, entombed, and buried on the property of a black sharecropper."

"Yes. I think. Maybe?"

He nodded. "Step one in proving or disproving your hypothesis is for me to see the coffin and examine the body."

A frown creased her lips. "Access is going to be a problem. First off, the dig site is an active crime scene."

"Wait. Please tell me the police haven't left the coffin out in the field?" Exposure to the elements wasn't going to do the coffin or its occupant any favors.

"No. Before I called the police, we moved the coffin to my makeshift lab in the basement of the Rutherford Museum. But seeing as how they confiscated my museum credentials a little over an hour ago, I don't think they're gonna let me waltz in and show her off to anybody—not even a forensic pathology consultant."

"Definitely a problem. But not an insurmountable one. Where is this museum, and where is the dig site?"

To his surprise, she gestured over her shoulder. "Next door."

"Really?"

"Yep, it's just back there through the woods. There's a nature preserve between the Sullivan property and the resort. I just cut through the preserve to come over here and work out some aggression." She waved the ax.

"Then the investigation is here, in this jurisdiction?"

Pennsylvania's municipalities, townships, and counties prided themselves on amorphous, amoeba-shaped boundaries. For all he knew, Alabama was the same, and the land next door was in a different jurisdiction.

She shrugged. "Yeah. Why?"

"That means your Chief Dexter is hosting the conference I'm here to attend."

"Okay. That makes sense, he loves hobnobbing. So what?"

"So, I'll make it a point to hobnob with him at the opening reception and mention my interest in the body a local archaeology professor discovered. I'll ask if I can take a peek."

"I wish I could be there," she mused more to herself than to him.

"I could ask him, but —"

"There's no point. I'm a black woman, accused of . . . whatever I'm accused of. And Margot Rutherford Sullivan has barred me from the museum. I don't know how you all do things in Pittsburgh, but you're in Alabama now."

She said it matter-of-factly as if it didn't sting. But her eyes said otherwise.

He almost pointed out that it was the twenty-first century. He caught himself. It wasn't for him to tell her what her experience was.

"Let's exchange cell phone numbers. I'll talk him into letting me examine the body, and then I'll call you and let you know what I think."

He held out his cell phone. She rested the ax on the ground, propped up against her shinbone, and keyed her phone number into the device. After a moment, a faint ringtone sounded from within her pocket.

She ended the call and handed his phone back to him. "Why are you doing this for me?"

Just as there were two answers to how he came to be in the woods, there were two answers to this question as well. "In part, it's professional curiosity. I've never examined a well-preserved 150-year-old corpse, and I'm unlikely to get another chance."

"What's the other part?"

"There's a Buddhist text called the *Sutta Nipāta*. It's a collection of stories that explain the Buddha's teachings. Anyway, there's one story about a group of monks who are being harassed by spirits in the woods. The Buddha tells the monks to show the ghosts lovingkindness and compassion, and then the spirits will stop tormenting them."

It took her a moment. "Wait. I'm the evil ghost in this story?"

He grinned. "I'd say an ax-wielding woman is close enough."

A real laugh bubbled up from her throat and escaped her lips. "Fair enough. You show me this kindness, and I won't chop you up with my ax."

7

Sully hesitated outside Grandmother's closed office door. She'd been in a mood all afternoon, ever since their meeting with Davina Jones.

He'd really rather not disturb her. But he didn't dare return Chief Dexter's call without first seeking her input. Truth was, he didn't dare do much without her prior approval.

His stomach dropped and his shoulders slumped, but he forced his hand to form a fist. He tapped lightly.

"Come in, Eugene."

He opened the door and shuffled inside. Then he straightened up and pasted on his game face.

She looked up, expectant. "Well?"

"Marvin escorted Professor Jones directly to the laboratory room, where she fetched a large duffel bag and a briefcase from her locker. She then asked to stop in the ladies' room. She changed into casual clothes, and then she proceeded to the employee door and left through that. Marvin thinks she didn't want to run into any of her students, so that's why she didn't use the main entrance."

"Then why is her car still in the parking lot?" Her tone left no doubt that she expected an answer.

The back of his neck prickled, and he had to fight the urge to turn and race out of the room. He tamped down his dread.

"I don't know. Marvin said she sometimes takes a walk through the preserve during the lunch hour or at the end of the day. Maybe she's getting some fresh air, clearing her head."

It was a guess, not an answer, and he knew Grandmother's views on guessing. He braced for her reaction, but it didn't come.

"She'll have to return for her car eventually."

"Yes," he agreed, unsure where this was going.

"And when she does, Eugene, you need to be waiting beside it."

"I ... I'm sorry, I don't understand. You want me to mill about in the parking lot?"

"Yes."

"But why?"

She clenched her teeth. "Eugene, did you notice the necklace she was wearing?"

He pursed his lips and pictured it. "It was a pendant . . . gold filigree with a red stone."

She blinked at him. "Are you being deliberately obtuse, or do you truly not grasp the significance—especially to you?"

"If it's real," he blurted.

A nod. "Yes. If it's real. So to answer your question, you need to wait for her to return so you can speak to her. Find out where she got it. Find out if she knows what it is."

"Me?" He squeaked. It seemed impossible that she would trust him with such a sensitive task.

"Yes, Eugene. You. After all, it inures to your detriment if it's what it seems."

He turned and glanced out the window at the lot below. "It's a moot point now. Her car is gone."

Grandmother frowned. "You can't put it off forever. The trust documents hold that—"

"We have a more pressing concern."

He couldn't believe what he'd done. He didn't want to hear it. Couldn't bear to hear it. So he did the unthinkable. He interrupted Margot Rutherford

Sullivan while she was speaking.

"I beg your pardon?"

"I'm sorry, Grandmother. But this is time-sensitive. Chief Dexter left a message for me while we were meeting with Davina. He wants to know if we'll underwrite the cost of a forensic archaeologist to examine the body. He's fairly sure Dr. Bean doesn't have the requisite expertise."

"I shall endeavor to act surprised."

What did that mean? Yes? No? Maybe?

"What should I tell him?"

"You should tell him nothing at the moment. I understand that his pressing concern is an examination. But ours is that necklace. And also the brooch."

"I don't know how you could make out any details under all the decades of dirt and grime on the coffin window. Wouldn't an expert help in that regard, too?"

She exhaled through her nose. "Yes, of course. But if Lewis Dexter can't afford to hire an expert, there's no harm in making him wait. Don't return his call yet. We'll see how things stand tomorrow."

He could think of *some* harms. But these, too, inured to his detriment, not hers.

So, he nodded curtly and turned to leave.

"Eugene—"

He paused, his hand on the door. "Yes?"

"Are you clear as to your priority?"

His chest weighed a hundred pounds. He sighed with great effort. "Yes, Grandmother."

8

Bette turned away from the mirror and wrinkled her forehead.

"I want to make sure I have the facts straight. You ran into a murder suspect in the woods. Said suspect was armed with an ax. And you offered to examine the body of her potential victim?" She stuck a gold hoop earring through her right ear lobe and fastened it while she waited for his answer.

"In point of fact, I think she's more a person of interest than an official suspect. But, yes, when you put it that way, it seems foolhardy."

A small smile played across her lips. "How would you put it?"

"I met a university-affiliated archaeology professor

who has some concerns about an artifact that was unearthed during a dig. My expertise in forensic pathology could help answer some questions about the age of the corpse and the manner of death, so I offered to lend a hand."

After a moment, she stuck out her lower lip and nodded appreciatively. "You must be a prosecutor's dream witness. That does sound less reckless."

"So you'll help me help her?"

"Help you how?"

"Can you introduce me to Chief Dexter at this reception so I can ask him for access to the corpse?"

She pretended to think about it. "Why not? It'll give you something to do while I'm sitting in sessions. I know you don't like being idle."

Bodhi lowered his head and brushed her lips with a soft kiss. "I appreciate it."

She leaned into him. "I hope you plan to show your appreciation more energetically at some point this weekend."

"I plan to energetically and enthusiastically show my appreciation as often as I'm able, taking into consideration your obligations."

"And I plan to hold you to that," she purred.

Seeing Bette when he returned to the room had

been a revelation. Her quick, impish expressions. The way she shook her cap of soft silvery hair out of her eyes. Her distinctive scent of rosemary, coconut, and lemon balm—a hand lotion the monks at the retreat center in her town mixed especially for her. Her husky voice. It all felt like home.

He'd missed her more than he'd realized.

He looked down at her. "It's good to see you."

She smiled up at him and caressed his cheek. "It's good to be seen."

Then she glanced at her watch, picked up her small beaded handbag from the bathroom vanity, and nestled her handgun in the velvet-lined interior.

After she snapped the bag shut, she took one last look in the mirror and combed her long bangs to the side with her fingers. "Looks like we're going to have to continue our reunion after the reception. We're late."

He held the door open for her, and they walked hand-in-hand along the hallway to the wide, wrought iron and oak center staircase that led from the guest rooms down to the reception area below. As they descended the stairs, mingled laughter and conversation rose over the sound of soft jazz music.

The lodge's large circular dining room teemed with small-town police chiefs and their guests. While

Bette checked in at a table near the open double doors and received her name tag, he stood off to the side and scanned the room. Most of the blazers, jackets, and sweaters sported a discrete but unmistakable bulge, and many of the women's handbags seemed unusually weighty for their size. He estimated there were upwards of a hundred and fifty firearms in the room. He was considering whether the considerable fire-power made him feel more safe or less safe when a booming laugh caught his attention.

A ruddy-complected man with jowly cheeks that hung down over a clipped auburn beard stood in front of the massive stacked stone fireplace that anchored the room. His head was thrown back as he roared with laughter. A small crowd gathered around him. Bodhi couldn't see the man's name tag from this distance, but then he didn't need to.

Bette finished up at the check-in table, joined him near the wall, and handed him a name tag of his own. He looped the lanyard around his neck and jerked his head toward the fireplace. "Is that man with the beard Chief Dexter?"

She smiled faintly. "Good guess. Some of these guys really like to press the flesh, natural-born politi-cians, I suppose."

"The chief sure is," he agreed just as Dexter grabbed a passing man's elbow with his left hand and pumped his hand with his right.

"You should've seen it three years ago when we held this thing in some itty-bitty town in Arizona. That chief managed to get the key to his city out of the deal."

"Geez, when's Onatah going to give you a key?"

"Key to what? A silo?" Bette tossed back her head and laughed huskily. It was her laugh that had made him notice her when he'd been investigating that garroting in Onatah. Her laugh, and her compassion.

"Should we go introduce ourselves?"

"He and I have met before. So, why don't you join that crush of folks at the bar and get us some drinks while I push my way through the crowd around Chief Dexter and get you your face time?"

"Have I mentioned lately that you're the best?"

She pretended to think. "Certainly not in the last ten minutes. Obviously, we're overdue."

She winked and started toward the chief while he swam through the crowd for the bar. Through his work in forensics, he'd spent lots of time with lots of cops, but he never really socialized much with them. Sure the occasional beer after a good arrest or a guilty verdict. And he always made a point of attending officers' retirement parties. But now, standing in a sea of police chiefs, he felt ill at ease and conspicuous.

He edged his way to the bar and ordered a beer and a vodka tonic. Once he had the drinks in hand, he dove back into the press of bodies.

When he reached Bette, who had managed to disengage Chief Dexter from his entourage, she turned and said, "Oh, there you are. Lew, this is Bodhi. Bodhi, Chief Lewis Dexter is the chief of the local PD and our host this year."

Bodhi passed her the glass and stuck out his right hand. "Nice to meet you, Chief."

The police chief gripped his right hand and clapped him on the back with his left. "Dr. King, Bette's been telling me all about your work with the forensics folks. Sounds like you sure know your stuff. Glad you decided to come along this weekend."

Bette tilted her chin up almost imperceptibly. The police chief didn't notice, but Bodhi understood. She'd already primed the pump.

He sipped his beer. "I'm looking forward to spending some time on these gorgeous mountain trails. But you know, I heard through the grapevine that you just caught a case with an unusual body."

Dexter grimaced. "Lousy timing. I was hoping to spend most of the weekend here with my brothers—and sisters—in blue. But the corpse was found on the Rutherfords' land. That's a powerful local family. Politically ... well, it's gotta be a priority."

"Maybe I can help?" Bodhi offered.

"Say what?"

"As I understand it, the body was uncovered during the course of an archaeological excavation."

"That's right. You sure do seem to be plugged into the local rumor mill."

Bodhi smiled enigmatically. He refused to lie. But if the police chief chose to interpret his smile as an admission that he had sources on the ground, so be it.

"In any case, I'd love the chance to examine the body. It's not every day an iron coffin from the eighteen hundreds turns up."

"Oh, now, I don't know about that ...." The chief trailed off and took a swig of his whiskey. "Our local coroner hasn't even examined her. He says it's a pretty delicate operation."

"He's right," Bodhi agreed.

"In fact, Dr. Bean says he can't do it. We're gonna have to call in an expert."

Bette cleared her throat. "You know, Lewis, Bodhi's

services are very sought after. He flies all over North America to consult on difficult cases. In the past several years, he's been everywhere from the Florida Keys to way up north in Quebec and my little corner of the world, too. The fact that he's just sort fallen into your lap here is a stroke of luck. You'd be crazy not to take him up on his offer."

Lewis Dexter tugged at his mustache. "I don't doubt you're right, Bette. But you know how it is—I don't have the budget for it. Heck, I've had to go hat in hand and ask the Rutherford Family Foundation to foot the bill to get a forensic anthropologist down here because the department sure can't. Not sure what I'll do if Margot tells me to pound sand."

"Please, don't give my fee a thought. I'll gladly do this at no charge—think of it as a professional courtesy. After all, I'm already here. And I've visited Huntsville's rocket center in the past, so I don't mind missing tomorrow's outing for the guests of chiefs. Frankly, I'd rather spend some time with that body than with a rocket."

The police chief belly laughed. "Medical examiners, you're a strange lot, aren't ya'? Though, truth be told, I'm not one to look a gift horse in the mouth. So, sure. Why not?"

"Great. Is there any chance the archaeologist who discovered the coffin could be made available while I examine the body? It'd be immensely helpful to talk to her."

That earned him a deep frown. After a moment, the chief shook his head and said slowly, "I'm afraid not, doc. In fact, she's ... a person of interest."

Bodhi allowed his eyebrows to shoot up to his hairline. "A person of interest in a one-hundred-and-fifty-year-old death? Is she a time traveler?"

"Well, now, see, I think you're gonna find that body is fresh. I've seen enough dead bodies. I'm betting that gal was killed within the last week. And that does cast Professor Jones in a poor light, for a number of reasons I can't go into."

Bodhi *hmmed* low in his throat and considered whether to push the chief or take his half a loaf and run. Before he could decide, he spotted the woman from the check-in table over Bette's shoulder barreling toward them. She dragged a large man by the arm as if he were a recalcitrant child. Another woman trailed behind them, but the man's broad shoulders blocked her from view. All Bodhi could see was a glimpse of honey-colored hair piled high in a loose knot atop her head.

Bette followed his gaze and craned her neck around. "I wonder what Jenny needs? I must've forgotten to fill something out."

"Maybe," Bodhi allowed, but he thought not. For some reason, the eager smile on Jenny's face left him unsettled.

"Oh, there you are, Chief Clark! I'm so glad I found you. You're never gonna believe who—oh, excuse me, Chief Dexter, I didn't mean to interrupt your conversation." Jenny flushed, flustered and uncertain.

"No worries, Jenny. You go right ahead."

Bodhi couldn't risk the chief using Jenny's interloping as an excuse to get away without firming up arrangements for him to examine the woman in the coffin. He angled his body so that the chief would have to walk right through him if he tried to edge off.

"Well, Chief, that's mighty kind of you, and you'll actually want to meet these folks, too. This here is Fred Bolton, Chief of Police for Saint Mary's Parish in Belle Rue, Louisiana."

Before Jenny could finish, Lewis Dexter was slapping Fred Bolton on the back. "Fred, how the heck are ya'?"

Fred Bolton finagled his way out of Dexter's grasp. "Great to see you again, Lewis." He turned to Bette,

"And I believe I met you a few years back in Oklahoma, right? You're Bette Clark," he drawled.

Bette smiled and shook his hand. "Impressive, Fred. It'd be more impressive if we weren't all wearing these lanyards." She lifted her name tag.

Bolton laughed. "Busted. There's someone I'd like you all to meet."

He and Jenny stepped aside to reveal his companion.

Her clear brown eyes widened and her face went white as she met Bodhi's gaze. His throat closed up and his heart thumped in his chest. What was *she* doing here?

Jenny piped up, "As luck would have it, Chief Bolton here is dating a coroner. Just like Chief Clark! I couldn't believe it when he mentioned it. What are the odds?"

Eliza Rollins pasted on a wobbly smile. "Indeed. What *are* the odds?"

Bodhi didn't know whether to hug her or shake her hand, so he did neither. "You look well, Eliza."

She furrowed her brow, clearly struggling with how to handle the situation. He knew the feeling.

"You two know each other?" Bette asked.

He coughed. "We do. Eliza and I went to medical school together. We hadn't seen each other for more than a dozen years, but we ran into each other at a conference in Quebec a few years ago."

Understanding dawned on Fred's face, and then he winced. "Ah, you must be Bodhi King. Eliza's mentioned you."

No doubt.

Bette threw Bodhi a puzzled look. She'd picked up on the tension that gripped the three of them, but she wasn't sure what to make of it. Dexter also caught the change in the atmosphere.

He leaned forward with an avaricious glee. "How nice that you two old med school chums happen to be here together. Did you know each other well?"

"You could say that. We even lived together for a period of time," Eliza's soft accent hung in the air for a half-second too long.

"Oh, roommates?" Dexter inquired.

"After a fashion," Eliza answered.

Dexter's phone rang. He scanned the display and took a few steps away from the group to answer the call.

Bodhi took a breath and explained to Bette, "We were romantically involved. It was a long time ago." Then he turned to Eliza. "It's great to see you again. I guess we're destined to meet at conferences, aren't we?"

"It seems so." Her eyes flicked toward Bette and back to him. "And it seems you're not destined to be on a solo journey."

———

Sully drummed his fingers against his desk while he waited for the police chief to pick up. Dexter answered on the second ring.

"Sully?" His voice was loud, competing with background noise.

Sully could hear laughter and conversations and muffled music.

"Is this a bad time?"

"Well, yes and no. I'm at the welcoming reception for the conference. I told you about it, remember?"

"Oh, right. The police chiefs."

"Yeah. Your ears must've been burning, huh?"

"What do you mean?"

"I was just talking about you. One of the chiefs brought her significant other along. Dr. Bodhi King. He's some famous forensic pathology consultant out of Pittsburgh. Anyway, he heard about your lady in the coffin and asked if he could take a look. Gratis. So, problem solved, buddy. Tell your grandma she doesn't need to loosen the purse strings."

Sully flattened his lips. The news did solve a problem, actually two. He wouldn't have to tell Dexter that his grandmother wanted to stall him on the request, and, if the coffin turned out to be a fraud, he'd be able to get rid of Davina Jones without a confrontation about her taste in jewelry.

But.

Dexter's tone toward Grandmother was unacceptable. Dexter knew it, and he knew Sully knew that he knew. Sully was obligated to chide him. But he and the chief had been dancing around an idea for months now. If he was ever going to wrest control of the foundation and its fortune from Margot, he'd need Lewis Dexter's help.

So, he ignored the jab.

"Excellent news. Just let me know when Dr. King wants access, and I'll arrange it. Any time after seven tomorrow."

"Will do. And listen, there's another forensic pathologist here, too. Another plus-one. They seem to be friendly. She might tag along. Dr. Eliza Rollins. Might as well give her name to Marvin, too."

"Fine."

Sully ended the call and allowed himself a moment of satisfaction. Sometimes things just worked out the way they were supposed to. He could feel in his bones that this was one of those times.

Before Bodhi had fully recovered from Eliza's cutting remark, Dexter was back. He pocketed his phone as he rejoined their group, then gestured with the drink in his hand. "Let's toast to old friends and new."

"I'll drink to that," Bolton said with palpable relief as he raised his beer bottle.

Dexter nodded and clinked glasses with Bette, and then he turned to Bodhi. "I've got a great idea."

Bodhi, who'd been trying to read Eliza's expression as she sipped her wine, snapped his attention back to the police chief. "What's that?"

"Well, you were just telling me what a once in a lifetime opportunity it would be for a forensic pathology expert such as yourself to examine this body of ours. Why don't you bring Doc Rollins along?"

"Oh, I don't know if Eliza would be interested in a busman's holiday."

As if.

At the words *examine this body,* all the awkwardness and anxiety faded from her eyes, and she turned toward him.

"What kind of body is it that you're so excited about?"

"A local archaeologist just unearthed an iron coffin that may contain the well-preserved body of a female from the mid-1800s."

"A body that's a hundred and fifty years old?" Excitement bloomed across her face.

"Possibly. Apparently, she's so well-preserved that local authorities think she's more recently deceased."

"As in within the last week," Dexter interjected.

"Bodhi, you'll recall I have experience with unusual methods of preserving and disposing of corpses."

He nodded. It was true. She did. "The turkey vulture men case."

"That's right," Fred chimed in. "She figured out those bodies had been buried for a year before they were dug up and picked clean. You ought to go, honey."

"Hmm ... well, it sounds like more fun than hanging around a spa."

Jenny pursed her lips skeptically.

"Amen to that," said Bette.

Bodhi took a moment to wonder how many

women shared his current and former girlfriends' views of spa treatments but quickly turned his attention back to the more pressing issue. Eliza looked like a kid in a candy store, Dexter was sporting a satisfied grin, Jenny was trying to make herself invisible, and Fred and Bette, well, they were behaving like perfectly reasonable adult human beings. He just needed to act like one, too.

"It would be great to have Dr. Rollins' expertise—and her company, of course," he managed weakly.

"Atta boy." Dexter pounded him on the back with such vigor that he nearly knocked his beer from his grasp. "I've already set it up. The coffin is right next door at the Rutherford Museum. Give your names to the guard anytime after seven a.m., and they'll let you in. Then you all can do whatever it is you need to do."

"Are you still an early riser, Eliza?" Bodhi asked.

"Not as early as you," she said with a faint smile. "But I can be there at seven on the dot."

"Good enough." He turned toward Dexter. "Chief, I want to be transparent. To examine the corpse, Eliza and I will need to remove her from the coffin. I have no way of knowing how quickly she might disintegrate once she's exposed to air—assuming she is, in fact, from the mid-1800s. It really would be best if the archaeologist who found her could assist with that."

Dexter shook his head. "I'm not worried about it, son. I'm telling you that girl's not been dead longer than a week."

Bodhi exchanged looks with Eliza. He could read hers clearly, and she was thinking the same thing he was: *We'll see.*

9

Washington, March 18, 1871

My Queen,

For that's what you are, love, you are the queen of my heart. I serve freedom, and education, and equality, it is true. But these pale next to you.

Just yesterday, the chamber had a long session. The gentlemen argued and debated, great passions inflamed, and the excitement rose, heating our cheeks. It was good work, love. Hard, good work. But I wonder if it is work that merits keeping me from your side, from the side of our young people doing their own hard, good work as they labor over their letters and their sums?

I banish these thoughts when they creep into my

mind. I take a long walk along the river or find a table at the library and read the wisdom of the Founders.

But, without fail, the doubts float back in at night in my chamber. If I could have you in my arms and at my side, how different my service for Alabama would be! It would be softer, fuller, and brighter.

When the Congress adjourns its business, I plan to travel home to check on the school and visit my family. I hear from the gentlemen that it will be in the latter part of April.

Will we use the same signal? Tie a red sash around the young black cherry tree on my cousin Jonah's farm to let me know it is safe, and I will come to you when I can.

Until then, yes, I must implore you to take great care. The reports of violence against the Carpetbaggers and my freed brothers and sisters worry me deeply. Do not think that those who oppose equality and freedom will hesitate because of who you are. Indeed, a gentleman from Mississippi tells me a teacher from Ohio was whipped and run out of his town.

Be brave, yes, but be cautious, my Queen. Do not let your fiery heart burst from those tender lips unchecked.

I am, always, yours,

I.M.B.

Bodhi found a quiet corner of the boisterous reception room, leaned against the wall, and tapped out a quick text to let Davina know they were both right. Chief Dexter had made arrangements for him to examine the body, and no, she was not permitted to accompany him.

He was slipping his phone back into his pocket when Bette strolled up and nudged him in the ribs. "Texting your girlfriend?" she said with a laugh.

Despite her light tone, Bodhi's gut tightened. "No, I was letting the archaeologist know that I was successful in getting access to the corpse."

She blinked at him. "Bodhi, I'm joking."

"I'm sorry. I just—" He let out a sigh.

"Your old flame's here, and it's got you on edge."

"Yes. But probably not for the reason you think."

She held up a hand like a crossing guard. "I don't think anything, Bodhi. We're adults—and middle-aged adults, at that. You have a past. I have a past. Whatever happened with you and Eliza Rollins happened at least a decade before we met. It doesn't matter, and it has nothing to do with us."

The way his breath caught in his throat made him think otherwise. He scratched his jaw. "I think it does have something to do with us. I didn't treat Eliza very well at the end of our relationship. I regret my behavior, and it's one of the reasons I was single for a dozen years. Until I met you—which was right after I ran into Eliza in Quebec City. My relationship with her is in the past, but its echoes are reverberating in the present."

Bette's expression shuttered. "I'm serious. I'm not interested in what happened when you were a medical student. People change, people grow. It's not anything I want to know about or care about. Clearly, when you saw each other in Canada, you reached some sort of understanding. Truthfully, I'm just glad you'll have another weirdo to hang out with while you're poking around the insides of a dead body for fun."

He managed a genuine laugh despite himself. He wasn't sure he agreed with her that leaving the past in the past was wise—or feasible, but he couldn't force her to care about it, and she was obviously changing the subject.

She must've seen his reluctance to let it go. "Heck, Bodhi. You're not the only one with a past. You don't think I have an old flame or seven running around this place?" She waved her hand toward the thinning crowd.

He made a show of scanning the assembled police chiefs as if searching for her former paramours.

When she stopped chuckling, he tilted his head toward the exit. "Ready to get out of here?"

"Absolutely."

They slipped out through a side door and into the lobby. When they reached the staircase, he put a hand on her back. "I have an idea. Why don't you go up to the room and grab our coats? I'll slip back inside and get two more drinks—if you're up for a nightcap, that is."

Her habit at home was to have one drink—and only one—in the evening, but she sometimes loosened her rules on holidays and vacations.

She nodded. "I'd say this weekend rates a second vodka tonic. Ask the bartender to use a light hand, though. Where are we going?"

"You'll see. It'd be a shame if you missed out on your stars just because we're not in Illinois."

Bette's grin was bright enough to light up the night sky, stars or no stars.

She kissed him and dashed inside while he headed back to the bar to get her drink. Given the morning he had ahead of him, he opted for a club soda. He met her at the wide front doors and she handed him his coat. He slipped it on and waited while she bundled into her coat. Then he handed her the drink, and they walked out onto the front porch, down the stone stairs, and out onto a cobblestone pathway.

He led her through the darkness toward the trail he'd hiked earlier to reach the garden. The mouth to the path was illuminated by small lights staked in the ground on either side. "I saw this great gazebo this afternoon. I think it'll do the trick. It's a clear night, and there's almost no light pollution out here."

They reached the small shelter perched on the edge of an overlook, and she exhaled, "Oh, it's perfect."

They settled onto a glider and tipped their heads back, opening their lungs to the crisp night air and their hearts to the bright celestial show above. She whispered the names of constellations as she saw them form before her eyes. He listened to the sounds of nocturnal creatures skittering across dried leaves, the wind whispering through the branches, and the distant burble of a stream or creek.

After a while, he broke the companionable silence. "I know you don't want to hear about this, but I need to tell you: Eliza and I were in a serious relationship during medical school and—"

"I've told you I don't care."

"I know, and I believe you. But I have to be honest

with you, even when that honesty isn't necessarily the kindest or most desired gift."

A shadow of discomfort passed over her face like a cloud. "Okay. Say what you need to."

He rested his elbows on his thighs and inter-locked his hands. "We had just found out where we'd matched for our residencies. I was staying at Pitt. She was headed to Texas. She wanted to stay together, have a long-distance relationship. I . . . didn't. I said that I was on a solitary journey. I hid behind right action, the prohibition against sexual misconduct."

She shook her head. "But Buddhism doesn't prohibit relationships. Obviously."

"Right. I was trying to make sense of a lot of competing feelings. I wanted to focus on my residency. I wanted her to do the same. I didn't see a way to do that and to give our relationship the emotional energy it would require, at least not in a way that I wouldn't deem misconduct."

He shook his head. His thought process had been so clear, so logical, all those years ago. Tonight, it just sounded lame, like an excuse.

"Shouldn't *she* have been the person to decide what level of emotional energy you owed her? Or, at least, it should have been a joint decision."

Her voice was sad. Not judgmental, not shocked. But sad.

"It should have. And I realized that—belatedly. That's why I didn't get involved with anyone else. Until I met you."

Her green eyes pierced his. Even in the dim light, he could see the intensity burning behind them. "Did you get involved with me as a reaction to seeing her in Canada?"

He took a long time to answer. So long that he heard her sharp intake of breath and saw her dig her fingernails into her palms. She was steeling herself for an ugly answer.

"No."

She stared down at her hands.

"Bette, no," he repeated. "Seeing Eliza filled me with shame, especially once I understood how much pain my behavior had caused her. I made amends. She forgave me—or said she did, at least. She told me about Fred. Their relationship was still new. I saw how she was able to commit to her work and to maintain a real bond with him. It made me question the stories I'd been telling myself for over a decade. It made me realize that connection didn't have to mean attachment in a negative sense."

She looked up at him and swallowed. "Go on."

"That's why I went to Onatah in the first place, for a silent retreat to meditate on all these thoughts. I wasn't looking for a rebound relationship. I wasn't looking for *any* relationship. I was looking for a quiet place to untangle my brain."

"And, instead, you found a murder victim."

"Yes, and that led me to you."

"The nearest female."

"No, it's not like that. I didn't get involved with you because you were *handy*. I think..."

"What, Bodhi? What do you think?"

He wrestled with how to express his feelings clearly. He needed to get this right.

"I think you have it backward. I didn't find you because I was ready for a romantic encounter. I was ready for a romantic encounter because I found you."

She looked at him for a long time before blinking and turning her gaze back to the night sky.

After a long moment, he did the same. He was looking up at the bright star cluster that formed Cassiopeia when Bette's warm fingers grazed his. She slipped her hand into his, and he wrapped his fingers around hers.

10

Eliza bent over the sink basin, splashing water on her face. She reached out blindly, waving her hand around, hoping to connect with a face towel. One was placed in her hand.

She patted her face dry and met Fred's reflection in the mirror.

"Thanks."

"Sure."

She could tell from the creases around his mouth and the tension in his neck that he was troubled.

"What is it?"

"What's what?"

"You're worried about something, spill it."

He leaned against the door frame and tilted his head. "You, 'Liza. I'm worried about you."

She exhaled softly. "Because of Bodhi?" She should've realized Fred would be concerned about her reaction to seeing him.

"Well, yeah. Are you okay?"

She shrugged. "I was surprised to see him down there. But, you know, Bodhi and I ... that was a long time ago."

"True, but I also know it took a long time for your wounds to heal. It's to be expected if running into him rattled you."

She reached up and unwound the elastic band holding her hair in place. She shook her hair down around her shoulders, then smiled.

"Two things. One, I just did this a few years ago. Running into him in Quebec City, *that* shook me up. It had been thirteen years, after all. This was less of a shock. And two, a certain police chief helped me speed along the healing process. My wounds are scarred over, nothing but a distant memory."

The corners of his mouth turned up, but he was not to be dissuaded from the conversation. "I'm serious. I didn't bring you here for a weekend of sleepless nights and panic attacks. This is supposed to be a romantic getaway."

She arched a brow.

"I mean to the extent the parish police chief and coroner can enjoy a romantic getaway."

She joined him in the doorway and looped her arm through his.

"Come on, let's have this conversation someplace more comfortable than in the doorway to the bathroom."

They curled up on the small loveseat across from the bed. She nestled into his side, and he stroked her hair.

"Comfy now?" he asked as she rested her head against his chest.

"I am. Anyway, this *will* be a romantic getaway, but the fact is you have sessions during the day. So actually, it'll be nice to have a friendly face in the sea of spouses and plus-ones."

"Is he?"

"Is he what?"

"A friendly face."

She took her time answering. "Bodhi and I made our peace in Canada. And he *did* save my life. So yeah, I'd say we're friends."

"If you're sure."

"I'm sure. You aren't worried that I still have feelings for him, are you?" Her cheeks heated. She felt like a thirteen-year-old girl asking the question. Besides, Fred wasn't exactly the jealous type.

He lifted her chin with his finger. "I hope to heck you don't have feelings for him because I'm wild about you, woman. But that's not what's worrying me. I'm concerned that working with Bodhi is going to be a strain on you. Stressful."

She heard the words he didn't say: *You've come so far. Why risk the anxiety that might provoke a panic attack?*

"I understand why you're worried, but, really, I'm fine. I can't pass up an opportunity like this one."

"Leave it to you to be all pumped up to spend the day looking at a moldy old body."

"Do you understand what it would mean if that body really is one hundred and fifty years old?" Her voice quavered as a jolt of excitement zipped through her like an electric charge.

"Honestly? Not really. I mean, I know it's very rare and all."

She drew a deep breath, but he cut her off before she could launch into a lengthy explanation.

"Do you want to play cards or something before bed?"

"Cards? I thought this was supposed to be a romantic getaway." She raised her eyebrows.

"I did say *or something*."

"Fair point."

She reached for his hand. They crossed the room to the giant canopied bed. Just before they tumbled onto it, he stopped short.

"Eliza, please be careful tomorrow," he said, suddenly serious.

Even though she was pretty sure his concern was for her mental status and not her physical safety, she chose to interpret it as the latter.

"Careful? How dangerous could it possibly be to spend the morning in a museum with a moldy old body and a nonviolent Buddhist?"

She knelt on the bed, reached for his shirt collar, and tugged him into the bed with her.

11

Saturday morning
Before sunrise

Davina dreamed she was riding a horse. She urged the mare on, reveling in the cool wind that kissed her face. Then the loud chirping began. She turned and scanned the horizon, but she saw no birds. The volume increased until, finally, it penetrated her sleep. Not a bird at all.

She muttered to herself and patted around blindly with her hand until she hit the snooze button on her alarm clock. Then she snuggled back under the covers to sneak in a few more moments of sleep before she pulled on her work boots and trudged off to another cold, predawn morning at the dig site.

Then she remembered. She'd been suspended. There would be no more mornings at the dig site. She propped herself up on her elbows and stared blearily at the clock face. Why on earth had she set her alarm for five-thirty a.m. on the first day of her freedom?

Girl, the least you could do is take advantage of it and sleep in until the new semester starts, she grouched at herself.

She reached for her phone to check the weather and saw last night's text from Bodhi King. She was instantly wide awake. She flew out of bed, turned off the alarm clock, turned on the lights, and brushed her teeth with one hand while she combed out her hair with the other.

She had no confidence that her plan would work. The only chance she *did* have was if she got to the Rutherford Museum's employee parking lot before the housekeeping supervisor did. She grabbed her phone, her keys, and her wallet and raced out the door pulling on her coat over her sweats. Coffee would have to wait.

She coaxed her old Honda to life and raced toward the long, winding, one-lane road that meandered up the mountain to the museum. When she pulled into the lot and saw that she was the first one there, she cursed. Too early. She should have stopped for a take-away cup of coffee. Her stomach growled in agreement. And a bagel.

She let the engine idle so the heater would do its job and watched through the windshield until she saw a convoy of vehicles wind up the mountain and trickle into the lot. When the familiar blue Subaru chugged in, she turned off the ignition, pulled up the hood on her coat, and got out of the car. She stamped her feet to keep them warm while she waited for her cousin.

Verna, sleepy-eyed and stifling a yawn, walked right past Davina without so much as a second glance.

"Verna," she stage-whispered.

Her cousin kept trudging toward the employees' entrance.

"Verna," she called a little louder this time.

Verna looked over her shoulder but didn't stop walking. "Who said that? Davina? What are you doing here?"

She jerked her head to the side. "C'mere."

Verna hesitated, pursed her lips, and looked around. She checked the time, then made her way over to Davina.

"What's up?"

"I need a favor."

Verna huffed. "I shoulda known. 'Course you only come around when you want something."

Keep your temper, Davina told herself. *You need her.*

"Please."

"You're too good to slum around with your family, right, *professor?*"

Davina ignored the sneer in her cousin's voice and focused on keeping her own tone even and friendly. "Of course not. Didn't I just see you at Aunt Robbie's place the week before last?"

"Girl, that doesn't count. It was Christmas. Even the most hardhearted fool sees their family on Christmas."

She had a point. Davina stared at her in silence. Verna would either nurse her grudge or would help her. It was out of her hands. She sure as heck wasn't gonna beg.

After a long moment, Verna sighed. "What's the favor?"

"Can you sneak me onto the cleaning crew this morning?"

"Why?"

"I need to get into the museum. It's important."

Verna narrowed her eyes. "So walk right through the front door. You're the head of the Jonah Bell Dig."

"I can't. Sully and Margot banned me yesterday. I

just need to get into the building for a couple hours. That's it. Please."

Davina's stomach dropped at the ugly glee on Verna's face. She could tell by Verna's eager expression that she was going to tell her no.

She hurried to add, "I'll owe you one."

"You'll owe me one. One what?"

Davina shrugged. "One. Whatever you need. Like a chip, cash it in when *you* need a favor."

At the word *cash,* Verna's smile reached her eyes.

"Actually, I don't need a chip. Sure, I'll get you a janitor's uniform and get you into the building. It's gonna cost you." She rubbed her thumb across her ring finger and middle finger as if the nuance might be lost on Davina.

"How much?"

"Family rate. I'll do it for five hundred."

"Five hundred dollars? Are you kidding?"

She shrugged. "So, negotiate."

Davina pulled her wallet out of her pocket and peered inside. She thumbed through the twenties.

"I have one hundred and eighty dollars on me. That's all I have."

"That'll do."

"Let me keep a twenty for gas?"

"Nope. I'm sure you have a credit card you can use. Run it up."

Davina blew out a breath, pulled the nine twenty-dollar bills from her billfold, and shoved them into Verna's hand. Verna closed her fist around the stack of cash.

"Here. Let's go."

"And?" Verna showed no signs of movement.

"And nothing? I told you, that's all I have."

Her cousin pursed her lips, crossed her arms over her chest, and fixed Davina with a steely look. "I'm waiting."

Davina almost said *for what?* But she caught herself. "Thank you."

"You're welcome. C'mon."

She trailed Verna around to the rear entrance.

12

Bodhi stood on the lodge's wide front porch and tracked the sun's slow rise over the mountains. The early morning stillness broke with the sound of the door opening. Eliza stepped out onto the porch to join him.

"Good morning." He turned away from the railing to greet her.

"Hi. I talked to the front desk, and they've offered to have one of the valets drive us over to the museum." She hesitated. "I know you like to walk, but it's apparently quite a hike. And the less time we spend getting there ..."

"... The sooner we can get our hands on that coffin," he finished for her.

She grinned. "Well, yeah."

"Driving is a great idea. Thanks for arranging a ride for us."

"Sure, yeah." She glanced down at her feet.

He turned his attention back to the band of orange spreading across the sky. After a moment, he said, "Last night was weird, huh?"

"It was. Unexpected, mainly."

They fell silent. After a moment, he said, "It's a funny coincidence that Bette and Fred are both police chiefs."

"Is it?"

"Funny?"

"No. A coincidence?"

He turned around and studied her face. "What else could it be?"

She shrugged. "I don't know. It's strange . . . I told you about Fred when we were in Quebec City. You didn't mention Bette. Why?"

"That's easy. We weren't together then. I actually met her right after that trip to Canada. I came back to the States through Chicago and stopped to see Nolan McDermott."

"Oh, Nolan. I haven't seen him in forever. How many kids do he and Katie have—two?"

"Yep, a boy and a girl. Anyway, after I visited with him, I headed to a meditation center out in Onatah,

Illinois, for a silent retreat. I met Bette when she was investigating a murder at the center."

"Why a silent retreat?"

He squared his shoulders and held her gaze. "Seeing you in Canada, it stirred up a lot of memories and emotions. Most of them related to how poorly I treated you when we were about to graduate. I needed some time to think about that."

Her eyes softened. "I think you should stop beating yourself up about something that happened—what was it?—fifteen years ago. I forgave you a long time ago. Isn't it time you forgave yourself?"

"Right action is one of the practices in the Eight-fold Noble Path, Eliza. I fell short."

"Isn't compassion also one of the practices?"

"Sure, right intention."

"It seems you ought to show yourself the same compassion you show other people."

He tilted his head and considered her. She was, canonically speaking, exactly right. "Thanks for that."

She waved his gratitude away. "Oh, look, there's Jason now."

A chipper man who looked to be in his late sixties stepped out onto the porch. He wore a fisherman's cap and sported a short, neatly trimmed, white beard. "Good morning, folks."

"Good morning," Bodhi answered.

"Jason, this is Dr. King." Eliza smiled broadly.

"Call me Bodhi," he urged the man as they shook hands.

"Nice to meet you. So, Doc Rollins tells me you folks would like a lift over to the Rutherford Museum. I'll just run around back and get the car. Won't be but two shakes of a lamb's tail." Jason headed off to the parking lot, whistling a tune that Bodhi couldn't place.

Jason kept up a steady stream of chatter as they bumped along the gravel road that led to the resort entrance.

"Have you been in the area long?" Eliza asked when Jason stopped to draw a breath.

He left the resort and turned onto the ribbon of road winding up and down the mountain before answering.

"Yes, ma'am. I'm originally from Portland, Maine, if you can believe that."

"Oh? How did you end up down here?"

"Well, ma'am, I worked at the U.S. Space and Rocket Center just down the road in Huntsville for years and years. When I retired, I realized Alabama was home—and not just because of the mild winters." He chuckled.

"Hmm ... driving us to the museum at the crack of

dawn doesn't seem like retirement."

The driver met her eyes in the rearview mirror and nodded.

"You caught me out there. After all those years of working in the lab, I found I couldn't just sit around and be idle. Some of the fellas and gals took up golf or hunting. Some of them went back to school and got new degrees. But I just like being out and about with folks. I get to meet them, hear their stories. Every day is different. There's no stress. No ten-million-dollar piece of equipment is gonna fly apart in space if I put a decimal point in the wrong place."

Bodhi leaned forward. "You were a rocket scientist?"

"Yes, sir. And I enjoyed it. It was an intellectual challenge, but there was a lot of pressure."

"I can only imagine," Eliza murmured. "But what fascinating stories you must have to tell."

Bodhi settled back against the seat while Jason told Eliza a rollicking story about walking an orbiting astronaut through the process of repairing a piece of equipment in a space lab with duct tape. He'd forgotten how warm Eliza could be. She was reserved —shy, really. If asked, she'd say she was an introvert. And it was true that big groups or large social gatherings had never been her cup of tea.

But she had a way about her that instantly put people at ease, made them feel seen. He'd always thought it had been a shame she hadn't gone into general practice or one of the specialties that would have put her in contact with living, breathing patients. Her soothing bedside manner and quiet kindness were wasted on the type of patients he and she saw. But she seemed at peace with her choice, so he let the thought wash over him and then drift away on the wings of Jason's tale.

When they reached the museum entrance, Jason interrupted his own story. "Well, here you are, folks."

"Oh, no, you don't," Eliza protested. "Pull over and finish your story. You're not gonna leave me hanging like that."

Jason obliged. He inched the sedan forward and pulled into a parking pad cutout near the edge of the circular driveway. "The short version is, the duct tape held, and the robotic arm worked until they could send up the part to fix it permanently on the next payload mission."

Eliza clapped her hands in glee. "Love it! Imagine working for the space program."

"You must have a lot of amazing stories, Jason."

"I think most folks have interesting stories if you give them a chance to tell them."

"I agree," Bodhi said.

Jason pulled a card out of his breast pocket and handed it over the seat to Eliza. "Enjoy the private tour of the museum. What a treat that they agreed to open the exhibits early just for you. Just give me a call if you want me to come back and pick you up when you're done."

Eliza thanked him for the card and slipped it into her bag.

They exited the car, and Jason tapped a short honk goodbye as he pulled out.

"What was that about?"

"Well, I know you don't lie, but I didn't think there was any reason to advertise what we're doing. Especially because we're not officially part of the investigation. So I may have led Jason to believe that we're just *really* interested in the history of the Rutherford Family and Alabama's agricultural heritage."

He swallowed a laugh. She was right on both counts: they should be discreet about their unofficial involvement, and he wouldn't have been comfortable being dishonest with Jason. They mounted the wide, low stairs and stood before the massive metal door. He pulled on the handle, but it didn't budge. Pulled again. Nothing.

"It's locked."

She checked her watch. "It's six minutes past seven. Do you think Chief Dexter's message got lost along the way?"

"Maybe. Let's check around back. There might be a staff entrance that's already open."

As they turned to walk around to the rear entrance, he noticed a rusted faceplate with a buzzer recessed into the wall beside the door. "Hang on."

He pressed the pad of his finger against the button for a long beat. Then he stepped back and stood beside Eliza, both staring up expectantly at the door. There were no signs of life.

After a moment, she said, "I guess we better try that rear entrance after all."

The started down the stairs, and the wide door creaked open behind them.

A man's voice called, "Are you all the pathologists?"

They turned and jogged back up the stairs.

"Sorry about that. I was just making my first rounds when I got the radio call to expect you. Come on in. I'm Marvin Washington. I'm the security chief on duty this morning." The security officer swept his arm toward the museum's lobby in a gesture of invitation.

They proceeded inside. The lobby was dimly lit,

the computer monitor at the reception desk was dark and silent, and the heavy hush that covered the space was palpable. There was no mistaking that the Rutherford Museum was not yet open for business.

"I'm Eliza Rollins," Eliza whispered her name, as if afraid to wake the building.

"And I'm Bodhi King."

They shook hands all around, then Marvin cleared his throat. "My marching orders are to escort you down to Professor Jones' lab. Her former lab, I mean." The faintest shadow crossed Marvin Washington's face as he corrected himself.

"That's right," Eliza confirmed.

Bodhi feigned a casual tone. "Did you know Professor Jones well?"

Marvin didn't bother to feign anything. He thrust out his chest and said hotly, "Well enough to know that what happened to her wasn't right."

Bodhi suppressed a grin. Marvin might prove to be an ally. "I only met her briefly, but I'm inclined to agree with you."

Marvin's eyes slid over Bodhi's face, weighing his words. Then he bobbed his head, but he said no more about Davina Jones.

He led them to a wide marble stairwell. They descended in single file and in silence. First, Marvin;

then, Eliza; and Bodhi bringing up the rear. The only sound was the echoing slap of their soles hitting the stairs.

When they reached the basement, Marvin pushed open the metal fire door and held it open for Eliza and Bodhi to pass through.

"Lab's down the hall."

They continued their silent journey until they reached the second door on the left and came to a synchronized stop. The door was gray metal with a small window set in the top. There was no nameplate or other identifying information on the door. Bodhi wondered if Davina's name had been removed after her suspension or if it had never been there in the first place.

He and Eliza stood back while Marvin flipped through his collection of keys to locate the one that would unlock the door. After jiggling the key in the lock, he pushed the door open and ushered them inside.

"Here we go. It might be chilly down here. Professor Jones always kept it on the cool side. But once they brought that coffin in, she turned the thermostat way, way down," he warned.

"Smart," Eliza mumbled.

Bodhi agreed. It was smart. Heat and deterioration

went hand in hand.

Marvin bustled around, flicking on lights, and then turned in a semi-circle and gestured toward a wide table that held a large metal box. "Well, there she is. Uh, I'm not sure if I can leave you and continue my rounds or if I need to stay. Nobody said."

Eliza cut her eyes toward Bodhi. Part of him wished she'd handle this question, given her willingness to shade the truth. But her gaze never wavered, and now Marvin was looking at him, too, waiting for a response.

He exhaled loudly. "I'll be honest, Marvin. I'm not sure whether Chief Dexter or your boss wants you to stay with us or not, but I know your time is better served taking care of your responsibilities than hanging around to watch us take care of ours. We're both certified forensic pathologists, and we know our way around a corpse. We won't compromise any evidence. So, you don't need to babysit us unless you feel it's necessary."

Eliza chimed in, "Plus, we're here with our significant others. They're both police chiefs in town for a conference with Chief Dexter. So you don't have to worry about us breaking any laws or absconding with any valuable artifacts." She tossed Hank a wink for good measure.

Name-dropping Dexter and mentioning Fred and Bette's connection to law enforcement seemed to decide the issue for Marvin. He jutted out his lower lip and nodded. "All right, then. I'll be upstairs, doing a walk-through of the entire museum before we open to the public at nine. When you're done, just press this intercom button here on the wall."

He pointed out the intercom box and waited until they nodded their understanding before continuing, "When you buzz the guard station, I'll come down to lock up and show you out. Good luck—or whatever."

They thanked him for his assistance. Bodhi waited until he left the room and the jangle of his keys trailed off down the hallway. Then he closed the door behind him and turned to Eliza.

"Unlikely to break any laws? Where did that come from?"

She shrugged. "Well, unlikely to steal any artifacts is true. We'll have to see about the laws."

Her smile was sly and edged with mischief, and he grinned back despite himself.

She rubbed her hands together. "He wasn't kidding about it being cold in here."

Bodhi turned up the collar of his jacket.

Then, in lockstep, they approached the table that held the coffin.

13

They stared down at the coffin in reverent silence, and the air crackled with possibility.

"Imagine if she really is a hundred and fifty years old." Eliza's voice was an awed whisper.

He tried, but his imagination failed him.

The torpedo-shaped coffin was dull, dented, and unmistakably iron. Patches of rust-red oxidization covered the surface in uneven splotches. He estimated the receptacle to be about five-and-a-half-feet long. A small window cut into the top of the coffin revealed a woman's face. The glass in the window was wavy and clouded with age. It made the woman look as if she were underwater, viewed through ripples.

"I read that these were originally shaped like

Egyptian sarcophagi," Eliza remarked, tracing a finger along the coffin's side.

They'd apparently shared the same bedtime reading last night. "Yes, but people found them disturbing and unsettling—the design made them think of their loved ones as mummies. So, eventually, models like this one were introduced—less ornate and less stylized."

"And less creepy."

"That, too."

"I wonder who she is," Eliza mused. She flushed. "That sounds silly. Of course, we wonder who she is. But this is different. You know, if a John or Jane Doe comes into the morgue, most of the time, with careful work and just a smidge of luck, you'll make an identification. But if this woman really is the original occupant of the coffin, her story's been untold for well over a hundred years. Learning her identity would do more than tell us who she is."

"Right. It would unlock a part of history that's been lost."

The enormity of it sent a frisson of excitement coursing through him. The flesh on his arms pebbled. He had goosebumps—not from the cold, but from anticipation.

"Exactly. So, how do you want to do this?" With the

question, her tone switched from awestruck to business-like. She reached into her purse, pulled out of package containing a pair of sterile exam gloves, and snapped them on.

He opened his backpack to retrieve his own gloves before answering. "Best practice would be to have a forensic anthropologist and a forensic archaeologist here. If I were running this investigation, I'd push for contacting the Smithsonian Institute for guidance."

"Absolutely. In an ideal world, you balance the preservation of the artifact with the examination of the corpse."

"But it's clear that the locals aren't going to go that route, and I think we can agree it's better for the two of us to do our level best to preserve the integrity of the coffin and the corpse than to turn this over to Chief Dexter and the local coroner."

The skin around Eliza's eyes crinkled in amusement.

"What's funny?"

"You probably don't know how right you are. Do you know anything about the local coroner?"

"Not really." He shrugged.

"His name is Charles Bean. Take a guess at what his day job is."

He'd had enough experience consulting for small

jurisdictions to hazard a decent guess. "Butcher?"

"Close."

"Funeral home director."

"Ah, you're getting colder."

He thought for a moment, "Taxidermist."

"Warmer."

"How about a hint?"

"He does work with animals, like a butcher or a taxidermist. But they're alive."

"He's a veterinarian."

"Bingo."

He considered the issue. "That's not all bad. A veterinary doctor may not know human anatomy so well, but he'll know pathology. And, assuming he's ever had to autopsy or perform surgery on a horse or a cow, he'd be able to do a passable autopsy."

She was shaking her head. "Dr. Bean has a veterinary specialty, and it's not large animals."

"Oh?"

"Fish."

"Pardon?"

"He treats exotic fish—exclusively."

"In that case, we may not be the Smithsonian, but we're bound to do at least as well as a fish doctor would. So let's get to it."

"I wonder how you open it?" She eyed the coffin.

He wondered, too. They rolled the metal table out from the wall, locked its wheels, and walked around it at a deliberate pace, examining the coffin from all angles. The lid appeared to be affixed to the base with a sealant of some kind.

"Do you see anything on that shelf full of tools that we could use to pry the lid off?"

"Like a crowbar?" she asked as she turned to examine the collection of archaeological equipment in the corner of the room.

"Yeah, or anything else that could be used as a lever."

"Hmm ... let's see."

While she perused the available tools, he crouched alongside the coffin to study the seal more closely.

The door to the room creaked open. A black woman wearing a hooded sweatshirt under a janitorial uniform slipped into the room. Her hood was pulled up over her head and she glided soundlessly in her protective booties.

"We're just about to start working in here," Eliza explained over her shoulder. "Would it be possible for you to come back and clean this room later?"

"No, ma'am, I'm afraid not," the woman drawled in a honey-thick southern accent. She pulled the door shut behind her and lowered her hood.

"Davina?" Bodhi peered at her.

Eliza spun around. "The archaeologist?"

The question was directed to Bodhi, but Davina answered.

"Yeah, it's me." She darted across the room. "I know I shouldn't be here, but I had to come."

Bodhi understood the impulse. "Davina, this is Dr. Eliza Rollins. She's the parish coroner for Saint Mary's Parish in Belle Rue, Louisiana. She has considerable expertise in unusual methods of preserving bodies. So she graciously agreed to lend me a hand."

Davina and Eliza shook hands.

"Sorry about the gloves. And congratulations— what a remarkable find."

"Thanks." Davina beamed. Then she began to bounce lightly on the balls of her feet, dispelling nervous energy.

"How did you manage to get into the building?" Bodhi wondered.

"I have a cousin on the cleaning crew. She sneaked me in with the staff this morning, but I heard Sully's here roaming around. So I won't be able to stay long. I just wanted to watch you work for a bit and be helpful if I can." She made circles in the air with her hand in a *let's hurry this along* gesture.

"Your timing's impeccable. We were about to crack

open the coffin, but maybe you know how to open it without damaging it?"

She gave the coffin a dubious frown, and then asked, "Do I need to put gloves on?"

"Better safe than sorry," Eliza chirped, pulling another package of gloves from her tote. She tossed the bag to Davina, who snagged it out of the air.

Davina wiggled first her left, and then her right, hand into the gloves, and then stepped between them to approach the coffin with a confident air. She squinted as she examined the seal around the lid. After a moment, she reached out and rubbed one gloved finger along the seal.

"Probably sealed with molten lead, possibly mixed with some sort of liquid or sand," she mused.

"What's our play?" Bodhi asked.

She turned a quarter-turn and motioned to the tools. "Could one of you hand me that crowbar?"

"So that *is* the best way to get into it," Eliza remarked as she hefted the pry bar and passed it to Davina.

The professor shrugged. "It's the easiest way to get into it." She bounced the bar against her palm, adjusting to its weight. "I'll use a light hand and try to minimize the damage, but it's an unfortunate reality that sometimes you have to break a few eggs in the process of making a historically significant omelet." She hesitated. "May I?"

"Of course. After all, it was your discovery." Bodhi gestured toward the coffin, and then he and Eliza stepped back to give her room to maneuver.

She slipped the bar under the top lip of the coffin and wiggled it back and forth until she'd breached the seal. Then she braced her legs and pried, levering up the lid. The tendons in her neck popped out from the strain, but after a long moment, physics prevailed. With a loud, slow, creaking sound, the left side of the lid rose from the base. The movement was almost imperceptible. But it happened. She created a gap. She scooted around to the other side of the coffin and repeated the process.

"It's loose," she said at last.

Bodhi and Eliza leaned over the table. Davina frowned. "The light's not great. Bodhi, there should be a flashlight over there. Will you shine it in the little gap for me, please?"

"Sure." He picked up a slim penlight from the equipment table and did as she asked.

She crouched and peered through the slit as she worked the bar. "A little to the right, and higher."

He repositioned the beam. "How's that?"

"That's good." She squinted inside for another

moment, and then returned to standing and shifted to face Bodhi and Eliza. "In addition to the sealant, it looks as though a series of springs or clips spaced about nine or ten inches apart keeps the lid in place. I'm going to work on one and see if I can trigger it to release rather than just prying the lid off with force. It may take a while, okay?"

"Okay. Do you need help?"

"Nope." She flashed a grin.

When she turned back to the coffin, he caught Eliza's eye. He lowered his voice. "Do me a favor and help me name her."

"Name who?"

"Her. The woman in the coffin."

Her eyes lit with understanding and her face fell. "I'm sorry. I forgot how you feel about words like 'specimen,' 'corpse,' and 'body.' Sure, let's name her."

"I was thinking Cassiopeia?"

Her eyebrows scrunched together. "Like the queen?"

"I was thinking the constellation. But I'm pretty sure that was named for the queen, so yes, like the queen."

"Sure. Cassiopeia. We can call her Cassie for short."

His flittering thoughts settled on the name. Cassie.

"Perfect. I propose we do a visual inspection examination of Cassie only. If we determine she died recently, we'll autopsy her. But if we believe she might date back, we'll give Dexter a preliminary report without slicing her open and recommend he find an expert to document her condition and to attend any autopsy."

"I agree that's the right course, but we're only here until Monday. Whatever expert they bring in might end up doing it after we leave. Are you okay with the chance we'll miss out on the opportunity?" she asked.

"I am. I'd rather miss out than risk destroying history."

"Me, too, honestly."

"Good. Then we have a plan."

"I'm in," Davina called. "I'll need some help easing this lid off."

They raced across the room and stood on either side of her.

"We need to lift it up and off Cassie gently. If we bump or jostle her, it could affect her integrity," Bodhi warned.

"Cassie?" Davina asked.

"We're calling her Cassiopeia, Cassie for short. Bodhi doesn't like to work on unnamed bodies. He wants to remember the humanity of the dead," Eliza explained.

"Okay, Cassie it is." Davina shrugged. "We'll lift it on three and put it down to the left of the coffin. It's going to be heavy."

Bodhi nodded. The iron coffin plus the weight of its occupant would be at least three hundred pounds. He estimated the lid alone could weigh seventy-five or more.

He placed his gloved fingers under the edge of the lid and curled them up, then waited for Davina and Eliza to do the same.

"On your count," he told the professor.

"One. Two. Three, lift!"

They raised the lid straight up about six inches, moved horizontally to the left, and eased it down onto the metal table with a muted clatter.

They gazed down at Cassie. Without the barrier of the thick, discolored glass, she looked . . . deader. The watery glass had softened the effects of death. But up close, her flesh was gray, mottled, and lifeless.

Bodhi'd seen several hundred dead bodies over the course of his career. He knew this woman was dead— whether she been dead for a century and a half or for a day and a half. And yet, she'd appeared like a princess under a spell in a fairy tale when he'd viewed her through the box at his elbow. He shook his head at himself.

Eliza gave him a curious look. "Are you okay?"

"Yes."

Focus.

He turned back to the table. Davina was fingering the neck of Cassie's blouse with reverence.

He pulled aside the stained and dirty cloth of the high-collared white cotton blouse Cassie wore. Eliza reached down and rubbed the fabric between her gloved thumb and forefinger.

"Even through the gloves, I can tell this isn't a blend. There are no manmade fibers," Eliza murmured.

Davina's head snapped toward her. "That indicates she's probably wearing period clothing."

Eliza shrugged. "Maybe. It's rare but not unheard of for a blouse to be one-hundred-percent cotton or linen."

"We'll have to see if there's a tag. That'll help date the dress. Although the style suggests it's not current. Who wears a blouse that buttons way up her neck like that?" Davina pointed toward the conservative neckline as she spoke.

Bodhi unbuttoned the row of tiny mother-of pearl-buttons as gently as he could. Even so, several of the buttons crumbled in his hands. The fabric fell aside.

They stared down at Cassie's exposed neck. Eliza's sharp intake of breath corresponded with a tightening in Bodhi's chest.

Davina must have felt the shift in the room. "What are we looking at? What am I missing?"

"Well, to answer your question of who would wear a blouse like this, I'd say someone whose been dressed by an undertaker or relative hoping to hide the fact that she'd been hanged."

"Hanged? How can you tell?"

Bodhi pointed a deep furrow that crossed Cassie's neck on a diagonal. "Do you see this groove running from under her right ear, down to her neck on the left? That's classic noose patterning."

"The rope would have been knotted on her right side. That's why the marks are deeper down here on the left and shallow up here under her right ear," Eliza added.

"She was ... murdered?" Davina blinked.

"She was hanged," Bodhi cautioned. "It could have been suicide."

"Or it could have been a lynching," Davina shot back.

Eliza made a small questioning noise in her throat.

Davina met her eyes. "You're going to say that you thought lynchings only happened to black people, right?"

"Well, yes, I was."

"You'd be right, especially in the South, especially right after the Civil War. Lynchings were common, and they were overwhelmingly committed by white mobs against black men. But during Reconstruction, scalawags—white Southern Republicans—and Northern whites who were sympathetic or helpful to the Freedmen were sometimes harassed, assaulted, and lynched as a warning to other 'race traitors.' It didn't happen often, but it happened."

"Would something like that have been reported? I mean, by the newspapers?" Bodhi asked.

"I wonder . . . I have a friend who's a librarian at the Bell Archives. He'd know if there's any record of a white woman being lynched around here. Maybe she was one of the teachers from up North who came to work with the Freedman's Bureau."

"Back up a second. There's an archive dedicated to the sharecropper? Did he have a lot of papers?"

"Not Jonah. His cousin's son, Isaiah Matthew Bell. Isaiah Bell was Alabama's first black congressman, and he worked with the Freedman's Bureau to set up schools for newly emancipated slaves. He eventually grew disheartened with the lack of progress and moved to Ireland or Wales or somewhere overseas. Like I said, I'll ask Micah. What else can you tell about how she died?"

Bodhi glanced at Eliza, who shook her head.

"What?" Davina demanded.

"An autopsy would show whether she suffered a laryngohyoid fracture, but we really need to get some DNA analysts involved. Now that we know that Cassie may have been murdered, we shouldn't continue to examine her. We might introduce trace contaminants," she explained.

"And we need to move fast. We don't know what effect being exposed to the air will have on a corpse this old or any DNA that's been preserved," Bodhi added.

"Good luck with that. There won't be any forensic DNA specialists," Davina said in a resigned tone.

"Why wouldn't there be? The case calls for it."

Davina paced between the table and the corner. "Don't you get it? They were willing to bring in an expert to prove me wrong. But to confirm that someone murdered a white woman and buried her on Jonah Bell's farm? No chance. They wanted a big splashy archaeological find, but this is *not* what they had in mind. The Rutherford Family is allergic to scandal. They'll bury Cassie—no pun intended—and me along with her, to keep a lid on the news."

"She may have committed suicide," Eliza reminded her.

"How's that better? They want a story that's all sunshine and rainbows, not one that's all death and devastation. Unless you leave out the part about how she died. Can you just tell him that you've confirmed she's from the 1800s? Then, maybe, *maybe,* you'll get your experts."

Davina's distress was painted all over her face, and it rolled off her in waves. Bodhi allowed it to wash over him, but he couldn't permit it to change his course of action.

He brought the truth to light. It's what he did. He would have to tell Chief Dexter what he and Eliza had found. Even if doing so would cause Davina pain.

"I'm sorry. I can't do that. The truth has to come out. But we'll try to get Dexter to understand how important your discovery is. And the Rutherford Foundation, too."

She opened her mouth—whether to argue or concede, he'd never know.

14

Marvin's voice, overly loud for some reason, drifted down the hall and stopped outside the lab room. He fumbled with the door for a long moment, then opened it slowly and noisily. By the time Marvin entered the room accompanied by a thin man in a suit, Davina had yanked her hoodie over her head, plucked a feather duster from the pocket of her janitorial uniform, and was brushing it over a bookcase in the far corner, her back angled toward the door.

"Doctor Rollins, Doctor King, this here is Mr. Eugene Sullivan. He's the Director of the Rutherford Family Foundation."

Bodhi thought he heard Davina mutter "deputy

director" from the corner, but a glance in her direction revealed nothing.

"Hello," Eliza said.

"Mr. Sullivan." Bodhi nodded.

Eugene Sullivan stepped out from behind Marvin and strode toward them, his hand outstretched and a wide grin splitting his face. "Please, call me Sully. Everyone does. And Marvin's somewhat overstated my position. I'm the deputy director. Grandmother retains the reins even at her age."

Eliza peeled off her gloves and offered her hand and a greeting. Bodhi followed suit.

Sullivan strolled forward and rubbed his hands together like a kid anticipating a birthday gift. "So, I took the liberty of looking you two up. Very impressive pedigrees. How lucky for us that two experts like you just fell into our lap."

"You're luckier than you know, Mr. . . . er, Sully. It turns out that Professor Jones was right. It's our preliminary opinion that the body and the coffin date to the same period. It's an extraordinary find."

Bodhi watched the man's face as he delivered the news. His mouth formed a small 'o' of surprise and his eyes widened. He leaned over the dead woman. "She's really been dead for a hundred and fifty years? Incredible."

Eliza plucked at his sleeve and gently pulled him back. "Please don't disturb her. Her value isn't simply historic. It's also forensic."

Sullivan dragged his eyes away from Cassie to fix Eliza with a confused frown. "What do mean, forensic value?"

Eliza glanced at Bodhi. 'You're up.'

"Just as Professor Jones' theory about the age of the corpse was correct, Chief Dexter's theory that she was a victim of foul play may also be correct."

Sullivan shook his head. "I don't understand. You think this woman was murdered?"

Bodhi used a pen to move aside the unbuttoned collar and pointed out the furrow left behind by the rope. "Yes. She was hanged."

"Hanged?"

In the corner, Davina was muttering again. Marvin cast a curious look in her direction, but she kept her head down and continued to run the duster over the bookcase. For a moment, Bodhi didn't think Sullivan had noticed her at all, but his nostrils flared and he beckoned Marvin with one finger.

"Tell the cleaner to come back later."

"Yes, sir."

Marvin's tone was perfectly neutral. A shade *too* neutral. But Sullivan didn't notice, and Marvin crossed the room and whispered in Davina's ear. She nodded, and Marvin piloted her out of the room, positioning himself between her and Sullivan as he did so.

Bodhi suppressed a smile and answered Sullivan's incredulous question. "Yes, hanged. Possibly lynched, given the time period."

Davina paused in the doorway to hear Sullivan's response, and Marvin obliged her by fumbling with the door again.

"Lynched," Sullivan snorted. "Don't be ridiculous. This woman is white."

Bodhi and Eliza exchanged glances. She cleared her throat and jumped in, trying a different tack.

"It's also possible the hanging was accidental or ... a suicide. We'll have a better sense of the specifics once DNA experts get involved. If there was a mob behind her death, there might be multiple DNA sources preserved on her body—"

He cut Eliza off with an imperious flick of his hand. "DNA experts? Absolutely not. The last thing we want is to undertake such an expense only to high-light the nature—pardon me, the alleged nature—of this woman's death. The notion that we would agree to broadcast this ludicrous theory is laughable."

Bodhi didn't much feel like laughing. But Davina snorted as she crossed the threshold and stepped into the hallway. Sullivan's head snapped up, but Marvin yanked the door closed behind him.

Bodhi stared at the man. "I guess we'll have to see how Chief Dexter wants to handle it."

"I guess we will." Sullivan's smile was thin and unconvincing.

15

Davina stopped in the basement restroom to try to lasso her wild emotions into something resembling control. She gripped the edge of the porcelain sink hard and absorbed the enormity of her discovery. It was almost beyond her ability to comprehend. Almost, but not entirely.

She was a bona fide Big Freaking Deal. And Margot and Sully were going to screw her over and bury the news. Bodhi and Eliza might fool themselves into believing Chief Dexter would do the right thing. She had no illusions.

Unless. Unless she beat them at their own game. She didn't have time to hang out in the bathroom. She needed to get out of here and call Micah.

She pushed the door open and spied Sully walking away from the lab. He was headed straight toward her.

Her heart thumped triple-time in her chest, and she turned on her heel and made a beeline for the supply closet to the right of the bathroom door. She grasped the knob two-handed, but her hands were shaking so badly she couldn't get the door open before Sully passed by.

She needn't have bothered. He didn't so much as glance at her. Deep in her belly, she felt a stab of the visceral anger that Verna carried around with her. But, mainly, she was grateful to be treated as if she were invisible. Explaining what she was doing lurking around the office museum in a cleaning crew outfit was a conversation she was happy to avoid.

And knowing Sully, he might have her arrested. That would lead to an even more uncomfortable conversation if she were searched. She snaked her hand inside the uniform's large patch pocket and removed the brooch.

She was confident Bodhi and Eliza hadn't seen her unpin it from Cassie's blouse and palm it. And they wouldn't have noticed the pinholes in the fabric. They'd been one-hundred percent focused on the ligature marks on the woman's neck.

She'd thought the round pin was special from the

moment she'd first viewed it through the coffin's window, still half-buried in the earth. But once she'd seen it up close, without a barrier, she could see nothing else.

She traced the intricate filigree that encircled the large faceted garnet stone in the center. It wasn't one of a kind—she knew that much. But it proved that the woman Bodhi had christened Cassie was significant in more ways than one.

She heard whistling and heavy footsteps and dropped the piece of jewelry back into her pocket in a hurry. She cast her eyes down on the ground.

Marvin Washington strolled by and, like Sully, didn't even glance in her direction. But, unlike Sully, he very much noticed her.

"He's in the boardroom with his grandma. This is your chance to get out of the building," he murmured, the words just audible.

She wished she could thank him, but it was better not to. She settled for a short nod and rushed to the stairwell. She was home free. All she had to do was race up the rear stairs and dart out through the employees' door. Yet, somehow, her feet took her in another direction, and she found herself with her ear pressed up against the board room door, straining to hear any sounds coming from within.

Sully's voice, muffled and indistinct, drifted through the door. "I explained that we would not be looking for any publicity about this corpse."

His grandmother murmured her faint assent.

"But they insist on speaking with Chief Dexter anyway," Sully continued.

Margot laughed, and, this time, when she spoke, her words rang out. "Leave Lewis Dexter to me."

Sully's voice rose in a question.

His grandmother assured him, "Lewis will understand his situation. He won't move forward with a criminal investigation into the supposed murder of a supposed one-hundred-and-fifty-year old corpse. It would be tantamount to tendering his resignation."

Davina pursed her lips and nodded to herself. It was just as she'd suspected. The Sullivans were going to sweep the corpse—and with it, the historic coffin—under a pricey Persian rug.

Margot wasn't finished, though, "Have you dealt with Davina Jones yet?"

"Not yet. The fact that the corpse and the coffin aren't frauds means we'll have to tread lightly."

"Not too lightly, Eugene. Pressure must be applied."

That sounded ominous.

She needed to get out of the building, both before

she got caught, and before she did something regret-table, like burst in on them Scooby-Doo-style to catch them scheming. She crept away from the door and made her way to the employees' door in the back of the building.

16

Pressure must be applied.

Sometimes, Sully thought, his grand-mother could be a tad dramatic.

She stared at him, waiting for some response.

"I'll reach out to her."

"Reach out to her," she echoed. Her upper lip curled ever-so-slightly. A display of cultured disdain.

She pushed herself away from the conference table, opened the credenza that held the foundation's records, and paged the through the bound volumes.

"What are you looking for?" He was much more familiar with the filing system for the organizational documents than was she.

She didn't respond. After a moment, she selected

one of the leather books, blew the dust off the cover, and placed it down on the table with a dull thud.

She flipped it open, paged past the index, and placed her finger on the page that appeared to be a formation document, either the charter or the irrevocable charitable trust agreement. Then she put on the reading glasses that hung from a chain around her neck and began to read aloud:

I, Louisa Anne Rutherford, being of sound mind and body, as the Grantor under this Rutherford Family Irrevocable Trust, do hereby proclaim that the assets herein shall be held in trust for the female descendants of the Rutherford family, for their care and ease, with the following conditions:

(1) The initial trust principal of one million dollars shall be invested and kept in trust in perpetuity. The annual income generated by the trust shall be divided as follows: (a) 25% to fund the operations of the Rutherford Nature Preserve and Open-Air Museum and any buildings constructed thereon for the benefit of the Trust; (b) 25% to the community in the form of grants and scholarships; and (c) 50% to the living female descendants of Louisa Anne Rutherford, per stirpes, to spend as they wish.

"Need I go on?"

Sully choked back his initial response and chose a more measured one, "It won't be necessary. I assure you, I am well acquainted with Louisa Anne Rutherford's grant."

Oh, was he ever.

"And you understand, Eugene, that your generous allowance is at my discretion, as was your father's when he was alive?"

"Yes, Grandmother," he gritted out.

"You also realize that I am, as far as anyone knows, the last living female descendant of Louisa Rutherford?"

"Quite."

She thumped the book shut and returned it to its place in the row. Then she braced her sinewy arms against the table and leaned forward.

"So, you understand that unless another female descendant turns up, the Trust and the Family Foundation, as currently constituted, dissolve upon my death, and your allowance vanishes with them?"

"As currently constituted, yes."

She gave him a sharp look. "Don't get your hopes up, Eugene. Louisa Anne's intent was clear, and I don't see a way forward to subvert it. No matter what your lawyer friends from Birmingham and Montgomery say."

"Yes, Grandmother."

What else could he say?

"So, it's important to get clarity on the brooch and on Davina Jones' necklace."

"I don't know about the brooch, but surely that necklace is a knockoff."

Another cutting gaze. "Reach out to the Jones woman, Eugene. I'll take care of the brooch myself."

17

Marvin escorted Bodhi and Eliza up from the basement and said goodbye to them at the front doors. Outside, Eliza called Jason to arrange for transportation back to the lodge, while Bodhi called Chief Dexter to set up a time to deliver their report.

"Jason's on his way," Eliza said when Bodhi ended his call with the chief. "How'd you do?"

He pulled a face. "He'll give us ten minutes between the breakout session on 'Rural Terrorism Response' and lunch."

"Ten minutes to brief him? Even though this may have just become a murder investigation?"

He gave her a long look. "I think Davina was probably right. I get the sense that the chief takes his marching orders from the Sullivans. If they don't want there to be a full-fledged investigation, there won't be."

The only way to describe her expression was *thunderous*. He almost ducked for cover, but Jason pulled up, so Bodhi hustled her into the car. They passed the short ride in ominous silence.

As they pulled up to the lodge, Jason commented, "I guess the museum was a let-down, eh?"

Eliza brightened for a moment before she stepped out of the car. "It wasn't quite what we expected, but I'm so thankful we met you."

Bodhi echoed the sentiment, glad to see that she'd cheered up.

After they waved goodbye to Jason, Bodhi turned to her. "Are you going to keep your cool when we talk to Dexter?"

"Keep my cool? Are you insinuating that I'm a hothead?"

He didn't answer. Instead, he deliberately dropped his gaze to her right foot, which was stamping the pavement. She stilled her foot and removed her hand from her hip.

"I'll be the perfect southern lady," she demurred.

For reasons he couldn't pinpoint, that promise did nothing to ease his concerns. But he managed a strangled *"great"* and followed her up the stairs to the lodge.

Dexter was waiting for them just inside the doors. He yanked the door open when he saw them approaching and hurried them over to a seating area tucked into the far end of the lobby where three over-sized club chairs formed a conversation pit. He gestured for Eliza to take a seat and waited for her to sit before lowering his bulk into the chair next to hers. Bodhi took the remaining seat, directly across from Eliza.

"What's your big news?" Dexter asked, glancing at his watch before he clasped his hands together and rested his arms on his thighs.

"Professor Jones is correct. That corpse is approximately one hundred and fifty years old."

"I'll be ...." Dexter shook his head vigorously. "I just can't believe it."

"It's true," Eliza informed him. "And she was hanged."

Dexter scratched at his neck under the collar of his plaid shirt. "Really, hanged?"

"Yes, hanged, possibly lynched." Eliza's voice faltered, and she threw Bodhi a look that said *'how about a little help?'*

"But, you already know all this, right, Chief Dexter?"

Dexter coughed in response.

"Mr. Sullivan called you."

Bodhi didn't phrase it as a question, but Dexter answered it anyway.

"It was Margot, actually. Uh, Mrs. Sullivan." He stared down at his hands.

"And she told you that the foundation wouldn't fund the forensic experts."

"That's right."

"I know you were counting on the generosity of the Sullivans to cover the costs, but you can't refuse to investigate a suspicious death because some rich family doesn't want the bad publicity. You'll have to find the money in the department's budget."

Dexter slapped his knee. "You're kidding, right? No offense, Doc. There's no money to find in my budget. Not for that sort of thing. Heck, we've got a whole panel devoted to stretching a department's dollars this weekend."

"Yes, but—"

"I'm running a shoestring operation. My coroner is a fish doctor. So if the Sullivans aren't paying for it, it's not happening."

Eliza flushed all the way to her hairline. Bodhi hurried to try to find a diplomatic response before she exploded. This was not his strong suit. He was a truth-teller, and he could be blunt.

"I do understand the financial constraints you're facing. But you have to investigate crimes. It's your duty."

Dexter bristled. "Thank you both for your work. I appreciate it more than you can know. But this is the end of the line."

Eliza jumped in. "The end of the line? When there's likely been a murder committed in your town? What about seeing justice done?"

"If—*if*—a murder was committed, it happened in the 1800s. I don't think I'm gonna have anyone to bring to justice. Unless you're suggesting the killer is the undead, like a vampire."

He guffawed at his own lame joke. They ignored it.

"But the historical record—" Eliza began.

Dexter grew serious. "I'm not a historian. That's not my job. My job's to protect and serve the current citizens of this town, not the ones who've been dead for over a hundred years. Is your Jane Doe interesting? Sure. Historically important? Maybe. But it's a cold, cold case, and there's no law enforcement reason to investigate it."

"Especially not when you're in the Sullivan family's pocket," Bodhi observed.

Dexter stood. He eyeballed Bodhi coldly. "As a courtesy to Bette, I'll pretend you didn't say that."

He strode off before Bodhi or Eliza could say another word.

Eliza exhaled. "Well, that's disappointing, but not surprising."

"True."

"Are you going to let Davina know?"

He should. But not yet. "Let's wait. We'll pick Fred and Bette's brains over lunch. Maybe they'll have an idea."

Davina trudged up the stairs to her apartment, unlocked her door, and tossed her keys and the stolen brooch into the empty fruit bowl on the kitchen island. She made a mental note to buy some fruit, flung herself into the chair by the window, and closed her eyes.

The original adrenaline rush that had come from learning that Cassie really did date to the Reconstruction Era had morphed to anger while she was eavesdropping on Sully and his grandmother. Then, during the drive from the museum back to her place, the rage had dissipated, leaving nothing but fatigue.

She felt wrung out. Drained. And bone tired. Exhaustion with a side of disappointment at the injustice of it all. She should be flying high, reveling in her discovery. Instead, here she was wondering if there was some way to salvage the find before the Sullivans buried it—and trashed what was left of her reputation in the process.

She toyed with the idea of indulging in a round of *life's not fair,* but her granny's words rang in her ears: *"You go and forget you're a black woman? What gave you the idea that life was fair? You get kicked, do something about it."*

She snorted. Stood up and stretched. Rolled her tight neck and shoulders.

Gran was right. And she'd definitely been kicked. Now she had to figure out what to do about it. She couldn't sit around and wallow.

Her stomach growled.

Food first; strategy second. She always thought better on a full stomach, anyway.

She used her phone app to place her standing Chinese takeout order, then she took a long steamy shower to wash away the remnants of her morning.

By the time she emerged and wrapped a towel around her head, she felt marginally less pissed-off and moderately more hopeful.

She picked up her phone to call Micah, the librarian at the Isaiah Matthew Bell Archives.

He answered on the third ring. "What's up, 'Vina? It's been a hot minute since I heard from you. Aren't you supposed to be working around the clock on your excavation?"

She snorted. "Yes, but no. I *was*. But I've been canned."

He let out a whoop of disbelief. "No way. What'd you do? Did you finally lose your cool with Sully?"

"Nope. I excavated a coffin from under a tree on the Bell farm. It dates back to Reconstruction."

"No crap? That's amazing. How could they fire you for that?"

"Long story."

"I've got time."

"There's the well-preserved body of a woman inside."

"Okay, so—that's what coffins are for, right?"

"So, Chief Dexter thought she was so fresh looking that she couldn't be the original occupant. He thinks someone killed her and dumped her in the coffin recently."

"He's a bit light in the brains department, isn't he?"

She chuckled. "You could say that. Anyway, you know the Sullivans. Sully and his grandma were all pearl-clutching and flustered. Can't have a scandal. So, they had to cut ties with me."

"That makes zero sense. What—do they think *you* killed someone and stashed the body in an antique coffin?"

"They don't rule it out."

She could almost hear his eyes rolling.

"There's something wrong with those two."

"You think? Luckily, Chief Dexter is hosting some conference of police chiefs this weekend. Two of the chiefs brought forensic pathologists or coroners or whatever with them. They're both experts in unusual cases. They examined Cassie today and said she's the real deal. A hundred-and fifty-year-old corpse."

Micah let out a long, low whistle. "For real? That *is* lucky. You oughta buy a lottery ticket."

"Yeah, well, the experts say she was hanged. And Sully and his grandma *definitely* don't want that kind of stain on their museum. They're going to quietly bury the news of the discovery."

He was quiet for a long, long time.

Finally, she said, "Micah?"

"I'm here. They can't do that. This is history."

"That's why I'm calling you, Micah. I thought maybe you could find out who this woman is and maybe get the word out."

"Who she is? I thought you said her name was Cassie?"

"Oh, right. No. That's just what one of the pathologists calls her. He doesn't like the dead to have no identity or something. But we don't know who she is."

"Hmm ... a woman who was hanged. Buried on Jonah Bell's farm. Maybe she was lynched. I'll look through the records of the freed slaves and sharecroppers Bell was close with, but I'm not coming up with anything off the top of my head."

"But she wasn't a sharecropper. She was wealthy. Oh, and she was white."

There were white sharecroppers in post-Civil War Alabama. But not many, and they definitely didn't get rich.

"Hold up. A rich white woman? Buried on the farm? That doesn't track."

"Maybe she was a teacher, working with the Freedman's Bureau. Didn't Isaiah set up a school?"

"Yeah . . . But, Isaiah and Jonah weren't tight. Isaiah was in Washington trying to pass civil rights legislation, and Jonah was a subsistence farmer."

"Still. Didn't the Klan sometimes lynch sympathetic whites?"

"They threatened to. There was an infamous cartoon about it. But . . . offhand, I can't think of local lynchings of affluent white women. And that would have been news."

"Can you dig into Isaiah's papers and see if anything pops?"

"Sure. It might take me a while. We've been archiving reverse chronological order, so the early papers, the ones from the 1860s and 1870s, haven't been indexed yet. Do you know anything about this 'Cassie' person other than the fact that she was buried on Jonah Bell's property?"

She sighed. "No."

"Well, why do you think she was well off?"

"Her clothes were fine, the coffin was made entirely of iron and would have cost several hundred dollars. And ..."—she scooped the brooch out of the fruit bowl and traced the filigree—"she was wearing a piece of custom-made jewelry that I *know* for a fact was expensive."

"Can you send me any pictures of her?"

"I don't have any. And there's no way I'm going to be able to sneak back into the museum to take any." She turned the pin over in her hand. "I can send you a picture of the brooch."

He clicked his tongue against his teeth. "Better than nothing, I guess. Text it to me."

"I will. And, Micah, thanks."

"You can thank me when I get you something."

"Drinks at The Distillery?"

"And dancing."

She ended the call feeling hopeful, almost triumphant. But Jones women were nothing if not clear-eyed.

Easy, now. You still have Sully to deal with.

She snapped a picture of the brooch and texted the image to Micah. She swiped over to her text conversation with Bodhi King to let him know what she'd overheard at the museum, but before she could thumb out the words, her apartment buzzer rang.

Her stomach rumbled again.

She hit the intercom and unlocked the door to the building. "Come on up."

Chinese food first; Bodhi King later.

18

Bodhi spotted Bette and Fred in the buffet line and pointed at an unoccupied table out on the terrace. The air was crisp, which meant there were few hardy souls eating al fresco, despite the heaters spaced throughout the seating area. It would afford them some privacy.

Bette nodded. Eliza joined the buffet line while he headed outside to secure the table. Once the others arrived with their sandwiches and chips, he went inside and piled a plate with salad and fruit, swept four bottles of water into the crook of his arm, and maneuvered through the crowd back out to the terrace.

"It's a little chilly," he acknowledged as he handed

out the waters. "But we want to be able to talk without being overheard."

Fred and Bette exchanged a look.

"What?" Bodhi asked.

Bette smiled knowingly. "Using my keen investigative insight, I sense this is a working lunch."

Fred nodded. "You two are up to something."

Eliza shrugged. "Guilty as charged."

"Let's hear it," Bette prompted.

Bodhi arranged his napkin on his lap. "Sure. But if you want to tell us about your morning first, we're all ears."

Bette arched an eyebrow. "Right. The panels are so fascinating that Fred and I have been debating the merits of finding a caffeine drip to keep ourselves awake for the afternoon sessions. So, let's start with your news. Spill it."

"The body that Davina Jones found almost certainly dates to the mid-1800s."

"Holy crow," Fred murmured.

Bette shook her head, in a fast, short motion, as if she were shaking water from her hair. "So . . . She's—a hundred and fifty years old?"

"Thereabouts," Eliza confirmed.

"Obviously, we can't date her with precision just by performing a visual examination. But we're confident that specialized testing will back up our assessment.

"And she's so well-preserved that Dexter really thought she was a contemporary corpse?" Bette mused.

"Yes. The relatively good condition of the body actually makes it easy to tell she didn't die recently," Eliza explained. "If she'd been killed and dumped without embalming, she'd have been putrid and bloated, skin peeling off, the whole deal."

Fred blanched and dropped his sandwich to his plate.

Eliza leaned across and stage-whispered to Bette, "Weak stomach."

Bodhi pressed on. "She's not just an old corpse. She's an old hanging victim."

Bette paused, her water bottle hovering midway to her lips. "Are you saying she was murdered?"

He made a *slow down* motion, palms out, urging caution. "We can't say that for sure. She may have committed suicide. But there's no doubt she was hanged, the ligature left deep furrows in her neck—they're still visible."

"Hanged," Fred mused.

"Possibly lynched, according to Davina Jones," Eliza added.

"We'd need to autopsy her to see if her hyoid bone was fractured or if any petechiae signs are visible on her eyes or elsewhere, but the likely cause of death was cerebral anoxia." Even though he realized the words were gibberish to the two police chiefs, he wanted them to have as much information as possible.

But they weren't listening anyway.

"Wait. Professor Jones was at the autopsy? Dexter told you that was a no-go." Bette's tone was mild, but her lips were ever-so-slightly downturned—an early-warning irritation sign.

Bodhi and Eliza exchanged glances. Fred noticed. Now he was frowning, too.

"Did you disregard Dexter's explicit condition?" he pressed.

"It wasn't like that," Eliza insisted.

"What was it like?"

"I texted her and told her she couldn't participate. But she managed to find a way into the museum and into the lab. Her lab," Bodhi couldn't resist pointing out.

"Chief Dexter's our host, not to mention the chief law enforcement officer here. You may think he's a windbag, but this is his town," Bette said.

"Bette, I didn't invite her. And we didn't mention her presence to the chief."

"Withholding information? That doesn't make it better." Bette's sigh was deep and exasperated.

Eliza cleared her throat and fiddled with her fork. "It's true, though. We had no idea she would be there. She apparently borrowed a uniform from someone on the cleaning crew and, um, sneaked in. It just didn't come up while we were briefing Chief Dexter."

Bodhi added, "As it turns out, I'm glad she was there. She helped us get the case open without damaging it too badly."

"Oh, well, why didn't you say so? As long as she did it to protect the historical value of the coffin, there's no problem with the fact that she trespassed." Fred's voice was thick with sarcasm.

The table fell silent. Bodhi sipped his water. He needed to get everybody on the same page, working toward a common goal—his goal. Sniping at one another was counterproductive.

He spread his hand in a gesture of appeasement. "Look, I agree that it was reckless for her to come, but it's done. The past is the past, right?" He locked eyes with Bette as he parroted her words from the night before.

She twisted her mouth, skeptical and unconvinced.

"I don't want to argue. And, besides, we need your help," he added.

"Aha." Bette unknotted her lips and smirked. "It's all making sense now."

"What kind of help?" Fred wanted to know.

"Chief Dexter claims he's not going to investigate the murder."

"What murder?"

Bodhi cast him a questioning look, but Fred didn't appear to be joking.

"The murder we just told you about, honey. Cassie," Eliza explained.

"Your Jane Doe from the 1800s?" Bette said.

The incredulity in her voice didn't give Bodhi a warm and fuzzy feeling.

"Yes."

Bette shook her head. "Bodhi, you can't expect him to spend resources investigating a possible murder that happened a century and a half ago."

"Why not?"

"Well, for one thing, there's no one to bring to justice. If she was killed, the killer is long dead, too, by now."

"I know but—"

"And for another, there's no family out there

waiting for closure. We don't even know who this woman is."

"So, we just forget about it? Let the Sullivans and Chief Dexter bury the news and move on?" Eliza demanded, her chin jutting out and her eyes sparking with anger.

Fred and Bette exchanged a look.

"Yes," they said in unison.

Bodhi inhaled through his nose, settled in the pause, and then exhaled through his mouth. He hadn't expected the conversation with Dexter to go well; he'd hoped this one would go much better. When he spoke, he chose his words deliberately.

"I understand there are budgetary concerns and practical concerns. But if this had happened in either of your jurisdictions, neither one of you would just close the book on an unidentified dead body. Murder victim or not. Ancient or not."

Bette tipped her chair back on two legs, her preferred thinking posture. After a moment, she twitched her nose and allowed, "I'd reach out to the historical society in town. Share whatever evidence I had and let them run it down if they wanted to, or could."

"And what if the local historical society—or museum, for that matter—didn't want to get its hands dirty? What if they directed you *not* to investigate? When then?"

"You know I don't take marching orders from a citizen, even a corporate one. But I wouldn't divert police resources for something like this. I couldn't justify it."

Fred nodded his agreement. "She's right. Aside from being off-mission, it'd be expensive and time-consuming. Why don't you contact the Smithsonian or the state archives? Ask them to take a look at your Jane Doe, er, Cassie. Or post an image on the Internet. Lots of genealogy buffs out there. But, while it's an interesting question and an unsolved mystery, it's not a law enforcement priority."

"And it wouldn't be a priority for you either if you were managing a medical examiner's office caseload with active cases that affect living family members. Fathers, mothers, husbands, wives, children, and siblings desperate for answers," Bette added.

Bodhi shook his head from one side to the other. What they were saying was true. That didn't mean he had to like it. But it was true.

"I guess you're right. It's just unfortunate. Davina Jones can't pursue it, not really. And once we leave town, we can't really drive the investigation forward. With the Rutherford Family Foundation and the local police department unwilling to pick up the ball,

Cassie will remain a Jane Doe and a potential murder victim. The coldest of cold cases."

Eliza scrunched up her face as if she were going to challenge him. But she didn't. Instead, she tilted her head and gave him an appraising look.

Then she said, "It is a shame. But I guess this frees us up to participate in the horseshoe tournament this afternoon."

Fred stared at her for a long moment with a skeptical expression. He might as well have had a thought bubble over his head reading *'What are you up to now?'*

Before he could express his palpable doubt, a waiter came by to clear plates and pass out cookies, coffee, and tea. They nibbled on the sweets and sipped the hot drinks, and the conversation turned toward the conference programming and Bette and Fred's upcoming sessions.

They continued to chat as they tidied their table and walked back through the dining room to the lobby. Bette checked her watch.

"Fred, we should run."

She leaned up to give Bodhi a quick kiss. Her lips brushed his, and then she said, "I know you're upset, but please remember we're guests here. This is Lew Dexter's town, not mine or yours."

"You're right."

"I'll find a way to make you forget about it."

"I'm counting on it. But, do me a favor and don't mention anything to him about Davina being there today. Please."

She hesitated, then nodded her assent.

Out of the corner of his eye, he could see Eliza and Fred having what was no doubt a very similar conversation, complete with hushed innuendo about the evening's activities. Eliza straightened Fred's collar and smoothed his hair before sending him off with Bette.

As Fred and Bette hurried off to their next session, Eliza painted Bodhi with a look. "That didn't go as planned."

"Not even remotely."

She sighed heavily. "What are we going to do?"

"I'm going to call Davina and let her know that we can't help her."

"Or ...."

"Or what?"

"Or we could help her. You and I both know she's going to investigate no matter what. We could give her a hand so she doesn't run afoul of the Sullivans and lose her teaching position, too. Do you know if she has tenure?"

"I don't. Back up. Bette and Fred just made it clear

that they'd like us to let it go. Are you proposing that we lie to them?"

"No, I'm proposing that we find something to occupy ourselves other than horseshoes. Look, all they asked is that we back off Chief Dexter. So we'll do that. Let's ask Davina if her librarian friend came up with anything useful. Maybe they could use our help. We don't have to do anything that would step on anybody's toes."

She twirled a strand of hair around her finger and studied him while he considered her idea. He had to admit it sounded reasonable. It *felt* deceitful, though.

She must've read his thoughts on his face. "Hey, this is our thing—an unidentified dead woman who may have been murdered. I can't just walk away from Cassie just because she's a cold case, and I know you, Bodhi. Neither can you."

That was the thing about Eliza. She was quiet, but when she cared about something or someone, she was tireless, impassioned. Unstoppable. And, just as he knew Davina would investigate with or without them, he knew Eliza would help her—with or without him.

"Sure. Let's do it. I never did care for tossing horseshoes."

19

Davina heard footsteps in the hallway and pulled open the door before the delivery guy could knock.

"I'm starving. Boy, am I glad—oh. I thought you were my Chinese food." She stopped and took a step backward into her small foyer. "What are you doing here?"

Verna stomped inside uninvited. "We need to talk."

"About what?" Her mind raced to piece together what could have happened at the museum after she left to warrant this visit.

Verna closed the door with a bang. "You know what."

"I really don't."

"You stole jewelry off that dead woman's body, cuz."

How could she know? And if Verna knew, who else knew?

"I . . . it's not the way it looks."

"Yeah? Because the way it *looks,* you used me to get into the lab to steal it." Verna's eyes flashed, and her hands were balled into fists.

Davina knew her cousin had a temper. She'd done a stint or two in the county lockup after bar fights got out of hand. But she wouldn't get physical with Davina. Would she?

Her eyes fell on her basket full of archaeological tools sitting just beside the coat closet. If she could reach the basket, she'd have ready access to multiple serviceable weapons—a pointed trowel, a flat-edged trowel, a wicked screwdriver, and a rock pick hammer, among them. Shoot, if she could reach the closet, her ax was inside, on the floor propped up against the wall.

"Don't think about it."

Davina's phone rang. She glanced down at the display. *Eugene Sullivan.*

"You told Sully?" Now Davina wasn't scared, she was pissed.

Verna blinked. "What? No."

"What did you do?"

"I saw you by the supply closet, admiring that pin. But, c'mon, you know I'm not a snitch." She looked wounded by the suggestion.

Davina forced herself to speak calmly. "I need to run some tests on the brooch. To establish a date. Margot and Sully won't let me near the lab, so I can't exactly test the body or the coffin, you know?"

Doubt clouded Verna's eyes. "Really?"

"Yes, really," she lied. "You say I know you're not a snitch. Okay. And you know I'm not a thief."

Verna's expression soured. "I guess that's true. Little Miss Perfect would never steal."

"I'm just borrowing it. I'll get it back to the lab without involving you. No one will ever know, and you're not going to get blamed. Okay?"

She huffed something that Davina chose to take as agreement.

"Listen, I ordered Chinese. It should be here any minute. You want to stick around and help me eat it?"

Verna's lips softened, but she shook her head. "Can't. Vance has to work. I need to get home to watch the kids."

"Some other time?"

"Yeah, sure. Some other time."

Davina walked her to the door and stood watching

as she trudged down the hallway like she carried a weight on her shoulders.

They'd never been close—and they probably never would be—but she could make more of an effort with Verna. She'd make a point of it.

After a moment, she closed the door and snicked the lock into place. Her hand was still on the knob when the buzzer rang again.

It was either Verna, with a change of heart, or the delivery kid, with her food. She pressed the button to open the lobby door and crossed her fingers that it was the latter.

20

Huntsville, June 3, 1871

Oh, love,

It is a kind of death to me that I did not see you when you were in town! I heard many reports of your comings and goings from the chatter of the men in the parlor, and yet I could not get away. Not even for an afternoon.

And, in truth, I was, I am, so tired. Tired and slow, almost as if I have a malaise. It must be the summer heat, but this sluggishness will not abate.

And now Mother has an attendant glued to my side at all hours of the day and night. And Rebekah, as you know, is gone. Off to marry and start her own life as a free woman. My heart is glad for her, of course it is. But this new girl, Mary, is a stranger to me. I cannot take her into my confidence and ask her to be my conspirator, not like Rebekah.

Mother's behavior was so strange. 'Tis almost as if she knew. But that's impossible. How could she know?

I have told no one, not one soul. I want to, of course. I want to sing of my love for you from my balcony. But I see now why you urge such caution.

A terrible thing happened here two days ago, not long after I heard that you departed for your summer house. I am sure the news will reach you eventually. A teacher from your school was threatened by a mob of Klansmen traveling through town on horseback. She was not harmed, but she was dreadfully scared and left town in a hurry the next morning.

The climate is so fraught here, my dear. I fear that the cloud of hatred and violence hanging over the green-tipped mountains will choke out hope, progress, and even our great love.

Oh, how I yearn to be wrong!

Will you be returning to town before your next session in the Capitol opens? If so, please send word, and I will endeavor to meet you under our tree.

Until then, I carry you in my heart.

Yours, always yours,

A.

Eliza chatted with Jason near the front desk while Bodhi pulled up Davina Jones' number and placed a call. A lawyer friend of his had once told him never write when you can speak; never speak when you can nod; never nod when you can wink.

The phone rang four times. Then a man answered.

"Please identify yourself." The off-putting instruction was delivered in a voice that sounded uncannily familiar.

"I must have misdialed. I was trying to reach Davina Jones."

"This is Professor Jones' phone. Who is this?"

Bodhi tilted his head, listening to the timbre and cadence of the speaker's voice.

"Chief Dexter?"

"That's right, this is Lewis Dexter. Now, for the last time, who is this?"

"It's Bodhi. Bodhi King. Is everything okay?"

His stomach sank. The Sullivans must have discovered that Davina sneaked into the museum. He hoped they weren't pressing charges, and he also hoped that

Marvin Washington wasn't going to get jammed up over it. He braced himself for Chief Dexter to tell him otherwise.

But what Dexter said instead left him gasping for air.

"No, everything's not all right. Davina Jones is dead. I'm at her apartment now."

"She's dead," he repeated.

"Yes. And as much as it chaps my hide to ask you and Dr. Rollins for help after the accusations you tossed at me today, I need to. Dr. Bean is at the beach for the weekend. And I don't have another coroner."

"Of course," Bodhi managed to croak through the fog that had seized his brain.

"Get here as fast as you can," Dexter instructed. Then he rattled off an address.

Bodhi repeated it back numbly and ended the call. He found Eliza still talking to Jason and nodded hello to the driver.

"Oh, there you are. Did you get in touch with Davina?" Eliza asked.

"Not exactly."

"What does that mean?"

"I called her, and Chief Dexter answered her phone."

She blanched. "She's in custody?"

"No. Worse."

"What could be worse?" She frowned.

"Davina is dead."

Eliza whimpered and swayed on her feet. Jason, who was standing just behind her, threw out his arm to steady her. She drew a deep, shaky breath. "What happened?"

"I don't know, but Dexter asked if we could come to her apartment. Apparently, Dr. Bean is out of town. Are you up for it?"

He eyed her carefully. Her eyes were enormous in her pale face. They were both accustomed to death, of course. But it's different when the deceased is someone you know.

She nodded.

"Are you sure you're okay? I can find Fred for you."

She shot out her hand and gripped his wrist. "I'll be fine. I want to do this."

Jason grabbed a bottle of water from the valet stand's supply. "You don't look so great, Doc Rollins. Maybe some water?"

She managed a smile and took the water with a trembling hand. "Thank you, Jason. That's very kind." She uncapped it, took a sip, and then turned her gaze on Bodhi. "Let's go."

He hesitated. It wasn't his place to tell Eliza what

she could handle. But he couldn't ignore her history of anxiety.

She seemed to know what he was thinking. "My panic attacks are under control. I'm not going to be a distraction." Steel edged her voice.

"Do you folks need a lift?" Jason offered.

He glanced at Eliza's set jaw and nodded. "Yes, actually. We're going to 1400 Pecan Boulevard. It's an apartment complex. Do you know it?"

Jason nodded.

"It's down the mountain and on the edge of town. We'll be there in about twenty minutes, give or take."

They formed up in a grim little knot and walked through the lobby in silence.

C hief Dexter met them in the apartment building's parking lot and sent Jason back to the lodge, promising that a black-and-white would return Bodhi and Eliza when they were finished. Across the lot, a female detective wearing a pantsuit and a badge on a lanyard around her neck flipped through a small notebook while a terrified teenager with floppy hair and a large earplug stammered out a statement.

Bodhi turned his attention away from the pair when Dexter cleared his throat.

"Thank you for agreeing to help out," Dexter said. Then he cautioned, "It's not pretty up there. I know you're pros, but I think a warning's in order. She was attacked."

The faint hope that Davina's death had been a tragic freak accident faded from Bodhi's consciousness.

"Noted."

Eliza nodded her mute understanding.

"Okay, so I'll fill you in on what we've got while we head into the building—"

"Who's the kid?" Bodhi jerked his head in the direction of the interview taking place near the shrubbery.

"Name's Calvin Wagner. He's a delivery driver for Chef Chan's China Place over on Magnolia Road. He found the body and called it in. Detective Valtri says he also lost his lo mein in the bushes. He buzzed up, she didn't answer. Someone coming out let him into the building, and he proceeded to the apartment. The door was ajar when he got there. And she was . . . you'll see."

"No other witnesses?"

The chief frowned. "Valtri has a uniformed officer

knocking on doors, but it's the middle of the afternoon on a Saturday. People are out, running errands or whatever. So far, all we have is Calvin." He gestured for them to follow him to a propped-open fire exit door.

"Officer Rey, this is Dr. Rollins and Dr. King. They're gonna help out with the body in Dr. Bean's absence," Dexter explained to the uniformed officer posted at the door.

Officer Rey stood ramrod straight. He was alert and tense. His demeanor was a direct contrast to the bored officers Bodhi was accustomed to seeing at crime scenes. It confirmed his suspicion that Chief Dexter's department didn't see a lot of violent crime.

"Yes, sir. Doctors." Rey stiffened.

"Officer," Bodhi said.

"Thank you," Eliza added as he held the door open wider so they could pass.

"Techs still gathering evidence in the elevators, Rey?" Dexter asked.

"Afraid so, sir."

"We're gonna have to hoof it. Four flights."

Bodhi and Eliza trailed Dexter to the stairwell and up the stairs. He was surprisingly spry for such a big, solid man. When they reached Davina's apartment, he lifted the crime scene tape stretched across the door, and they ducked underneath.

Bodhi sucked in a breath. Dexter had been right: the scene was gruesome.

Davina's lifeless body was splayed across the narrow hallway just beyond her kitchen. Signs of a struggle were everywhere. A ceramic fruit bowl lay shattered, its shards scattered across the tile floor. A set of keys was wedged under the refrigerator. Beside the refrigerator, a nine-inch chef's knife protruded from the wall. And a basket of archaeological tools was tipped over next to the closet—spades and trowels, rock pick hammers and chisels, and brushes were strewn nearby.

"There's no mystery about the murder weapon," Dexter observed needlessly. A long-handled screwdriver protruded from Davina's right thigh.

"No, no mystery there," Bodhi agreed. He eyed her blood-soaked pant leg and the pool of blood that slicked the floor around her prone form. "And no mystery as to cause of death either."

"Exsanguination due to femoral arterial hemorrhage," Eliza said softly.

"Almost certainly."

"What's that?" Dexter asked.

"In plain English, she was stabbed through her

femoral artery and bled out," Bodhi explained. "Rapid, extensive blood loss. I expect an autopsy will confirm it."

Eliza knelt and gently lifted each of Davina's hands, turning them palm up to show him. "No defensive injuries."

"What do you make of the knife in the wall?" Dexter asked.

Bodhi squinted at the knife sticking out of the wall near the refrigerator. "I think Davina threw it at her assailant."

"She threw it?" Dexter repeated.

"She was an ax-thrower for sport or fitness or, I don't know, maybe just fun." Bodhi surveyed the room. "I think she first tried to reach something in the fruit bowl—"

"Keys, maybe? That's where I keep mine. Hers are under the refrigerator," Eliza observed.

"That tracks. She's reaching for her keys—maybe to run, maybe to use as a weapon—and she knocks over the bowl. It crashes to the ground and startles the intruder, who hasn't advanced past the refrigerator at this point. Davina grabs a knife from the knife block, chucks it at her attacker, and misses. So she ran for her basket of tools, but the bad actor got there first."

"Would've been smarter to hang onto the knife."

He bristled at Dexter's second-guessing. He took note of his reaction and allowed it to pass. "Maybe," he allowed. "Well, sure, clearly, in retrospect. She would've had a fighting chance. But she was a fairly expert thrower. I watched her hit a tree stump from twenty feet at least a dozen times in a row yesterday. She probably liked her odds of taking out her assailant without getting too close. She likely miscalculated for the lighter weight and closer distance."

"Presumably, she knew her killer, right? She let them into the apartment," Eliza mused, still kneeling beside Davina.

Bodhi watched with concern as she smoothed back Davina's hair. You didn't have to be a Buddhist to know that emotional attachment to a corpse was inadvisable.

Dexter shook his head and answered Eliza before Bodhi could intervene in her ministrations to Davina's body.

"Maybe, but maybe not. She was expecting her Chinese food, and Calvin said she was a regular. She usually buzzed him up without asking him to identify himself. She might have thought it was her Szechuan shrimp and broccoli and not a murderer when she opened the door. We'll know more once we have a better timeline of her last hours."

Bodhi and Eliza exchanged heavy looks. They had to tell him that Davina had been at the museum earlier. It was critical to piecing together an accurate account of her whereabouts during her final hours.

"It's obvious you have something to say. Out with it."

"Professor Jones was at the Rutherford Museum this morning."

"Not possible. The Sullivans suspended her and banned her from the premises."

"True, but she wanted to be there when we examined Cassie—that's what we're calling the Jane Doe," Bodhi explained.

"We didn't invite her, and we didn't know she was coming, but she showed up," Eliza said.

"How'd she get past security?"

"She sneaked in with the cleaning crew." Bodhi saw no reason to mention that the head of security was well aware that she'd done so.

"Just great. Now, we're going to have to talk to Margot and Sully." Dexter scowled.

A suited-up tech came and stood about a foot behind Dexter. He was holding a silver smartphone. "Chief?"

"What?" Dexter snapped as he turned.

"I got into her activity log. She has a missed call

from Eugene Sullivan, but he didn't leave a message. She also made one phone call today. The number belongs to a Micah Birch. We're running down his last known address, but the phone bill is paid by the Isaiah Bell Archives."

The librarian. She'd called and asked him for help.

"Just one call? What about her Chinese food?" Eliza asked.

"She placed the order through an app on her phone."

"What time was that?"

"She ordered the food at eleven-thirty and placed the call twenty-two minutes later. The shower is wet, and there's a damp towel hanging over her towel bar. She probably showered in between."

"Or the killer did, afterward," Dexter mused. "How likely is it that they got blood on them?"

"Highly," Bodhi answered.

"It was her. The shower, I mean. Her hair is still damp ... and I can smell soap and shampoo." Eliza's voice wobbled in the middle of the sentence, but she cleared her throat and finished firmly.

"Thanks, Clive. Why don't you all finish up here while I call Sully and make an appointment?" Dexter didn't wait for an answer. He stepped out into the hall with his head bent over his phone.

"Clive, would you mind taking a photograph of this basket of tools?" Bodhi asked. "I need to confirm something."

Eliza furrowed her brow at the request.

"Sure," Clive said. He rested Davina's phone on the edge of the kitchen island and crouched to snap several closeup pictures of the basket.

Bodhi stared at Eliza and jerked his head toward the phone. Understanding dawned in her eyes, and she lined up her own phone with Davina's activity log and snapped a picture of the screen.

Clive stood. "That should do it."

"Thanks," Bodhi said.

"Oh, here, don't forget Professor Jones' phone," Eliza chirped, passing it to him with a helpful smile.

21

Lewis Dexter was grim-faced and quiet during the drive to the museum from Davina Jones' apartment. The uniformed officer chauffeuring them in the chief's black sedan glanced nervously in the rearview mirror several times, catching Bodhi's eye.

Bodhi sensed the officer wanted to make sure he and Eliza knew that he, too, was uncomfortable with the stony silence. He flashed a small smile of solidarity.

Finally, Eliza broke the spell. "I'm sorry you're missing so much of your conference, Chief."

He shrugged and stroked his beard, then he twisted around in his seat to peer at Eliza and Bodhi. "Duty calls. I'm sure you folks know that more than most. And again, I sure do appreciate your help on this."

"Of course," Eliza said.

Bodhi nodded. There was nothing sincere about Dexter's supposed gratitude—his affect was flat and toneless. But Bodhi was impressed that he managed to leave unsaid *'even if you don't seem to be able to follow my ground rules.'*

For the second time in eight hours, Bodhi and Eliza rolled through the property's scrollwork gate and arrived at the front entrance of the Rutherford Museum. When the car was parallel with the museum doors, the uniformed officer parked and jumped out so quickly that Bodhi started. But he was only running around to open the door for Eliza as if he were a proper chauffeur.

"Thank you, Officer Kincaid."

Bodhi smiled to himself. Dexter hadn't introduced his driver, and, if Officer Kincaid had introduced himself, he'd missed it. But he suspected Eliza had made it a point to check his badge. Just as it was important to him to name the dead, it was important to her to name and recognize the living. He thanked the officer as he exited the car and joined the police chief and Eliza in front of the museum.

Marvin Washington waited for them in an alcove to the right of the door.

"Chief, Doctors, I'm to escort you up to Mrs. Sullivan's office."

Dexter frowned. "Where's Sully?"

"He's already up there meeting with Mrs. Sullivan."

Dexter pulled out his phone and spent the walk to the elevator lobby reading his messages. Eliza kept pace with him, so Bodhi fell back and slowed his stride.

"How are you holding up, Marvin?"

"Just fine, sir." He answered in an impersonal, official tone.

Bodhi gave him a close look. "Come on, Marvin. I can tell you considered Davina a friend, and I know you helped her—or, at least, didn't give her away—when she sneaked into the lab to work with Dr. Rollins and me."

Marvin opened his mouth, but Bodhi stopped him before he could deny it.

"Don't misunderstand. I'm *glad* she was there. Her expertise was valuable to our evaluation, and, more than that, she deserved to be there."

Marvin's rigid shoulders relaxed half an inch. He nodded.

Bodhi went on, "I don't intend to tell Mr. Sullivan or his grandmother about your involvement, such as it was."

Marvin's shoulders drooped, going from relaxed to dejected. "You have to."

"No. It's not necessary."

"I'm not going to impede an investigation into Professor Jones' death. No sir. And, I didn't help her sneak in. But, when I saw her, I looked the other way. And . . . I helped her sneak out. I'd do it again." His chin jutted out. Then doubt flickered in his eyes. "Unless that's what got her killed."

"Let's not get ahead of ourselves. Your integrity is commendable, but there's no need to jeopardize your position here. Dr. Rollins and I are here to explain that Davina was in the museum today. We can do that without mentioning you." It wasn't lying, he reasoned. It was withholding irrelevant information.

"I appreciate that. And if you want to do that, that's your choice. But if I have to come clean, I will. I've got a good pension. This is just something to keep me busy, and I happen to love history."

Bodhi eyed him. "Are you former law enforcement?"

"Nope. Close, though. Retired U.S. Army. I'll be just fine with or without this job." His expression tightened. "I sure hope they can catch the devil who did this to Davina. That's the only thing that matters."

"It's clear Davina's working relationship with the Sullivans didn't end on a positive note. Is there any chance Sully—?"

Marvin glanced ahead at the chief's back before answering. "Nah, I can't see him stabbing someone. At least not with a literal screwdriver. Now a metaphorical knife in the back? That's definitely his speed."

They shared a chuckle.

"What about his grandmother?"

"Mrs. Sullivan? She's gotta be what, in her late seventies? Maybe older."

Bodhi shrugged. "You'd be surprised what people are capable of. Even sweet senior citizens."

"Hang on now. There's nothing *sweet* about Margot Rutherford Sullivan. She's a tough bird. But a killer?" Marvin dismissed the idea with a shake of his head.

"Well, as between the two of them, who do you like better for it?"

Marvin scratched his ear. "Between that pair? I put my money on her. But I don't think it was either one of them. They don't generally get their own hands dirty."

"I know Sully was here this morning. Was Mrs. Sullivan?"

"Yes, she was. In fact, she was here early. Even

before you and Dr. Rollins came. She asked me to show her the coffin."

"Did you?"

"Sure. It's her museum. She didn't touch anything, and she didn't stay long. You know, it's so cold in that lab. She just leaned in real close, peering into the window. She seemed more interested in the woman's jewelry than in the woman or the coffin, truth be told." He raised one shoulder in a half shrug.

Bodhi searched his memory. He was sure he and Eliza hadn't cataloged any jewelry.

"What jewelry?"

"Some kind of ornate pin. Right here." He pointed to the base of his throat.

Bodhi would be surprised if he and Eliza had missed something so obvious. He'd have to remember to ask her.

"Huh. Any idea if either Sully or Mrs. Sullivan left for a while, maybe around lunchtime?"

"Couldn't rightly say. I was taking care of . . . an issue at that time, so I wasn't at the security desk."

"This issue, was it related to the coffin in any way?"

"Sorta. It's going to come out eventually. I'm sure Sully and Margot are just bursting to tell Chief Dexter all about it. So, you know Davina asked her cousin

Verna to help sneak her on to the cleaning crew, right?"

"Yes."

"When Verna found out that Davina had left without doing any actual cleaning or finishing the shift, she lost it, causing a ruckus in the staff break room—yelling and hollering about putting her neck out for her 'uppity' cousin, who, in Verna's words, had 'done her dirty.' One of the janitorial staff radioed for me because Verna was punching walls and screaming."

"That seems like a disproportionate response."

"I thought so, too. I tried to calm her down and explained that I had seen her cousin in the hall and told her to leave, which is true. I let Verna think I'd kicked her out. That seemed to give her some satisfaction, but then she got worried that her role in the whole thing would come out. I told her to go home and calm down. I assured her I'd talk to the staff supervisor when she comes in on Monday and make sure Verna got paid for a full day."

"But she's still probably going to be disciplined for helping Davina?"

Marvin nodded. "Probably. And she was still plenty worked up when she left and convinced she was going to get fired over it. I don't think that means she stabbed Davina. But someone did, and people *have* killed for less. I'm sure I don't need to tell you that."

Just then, Eliza called across the atrium. "The elevator's here."

Bodhi shook Marvin's hand. "Thanks for the information."

"Anything I can do to help. I mean it. Here, hang on." He slipped a business card out of his wallet and scrawled a phone number on the back. "Call this number, any time day or night, if you need anything."

He took the card and met the security guard's sorrowful hazel eyes. "I will," he promised.

Then he tucked the card into his own wallet, and they hurried across the lobby to join the others at the elevator bank.

22

Sully watched as his grandmother decided how much she wanted to know. He thought— hoped—her legendary gentility would win out and she would refrain from asking sticky questions.

She turned the brooch over in her hand. "And you say Davina's cousin gave this to you?"

"Yes."

She tore her attention away from the jewelry in her hand. "Elaborate, please."

Shoot. Apparently, curiosity trumped refinement in this instance.

He took his time framing his explanation. Then he said, "I called Davina, per your request, but she didn't answer. Because I knew it was important to you, I decided to visit her in person. At her apartment, I parked in the lot next to a blue Subaru with a Rutherford Museum parking pass. Obviously, it wasn't Davina's. She drives, er, drove that run-down Honda."

"Obviously."

"I called Marvin to find out whose car it was, and he looked up the parking pass number. It came back to Verna Martin. That's when he told me that the two women are cousins. Verna's on the cleaning crew."

"Go on."

"I was sitting out in my car, trying to decide whether to go forward with my visit or wait until Davina's cousin left. I saw an agitated looking woman rush out of the building and run toward the Subaru. She seemed quite distressed, so I got out and introduced myself."

"She knew who you were, of course."

He nodded. "Of course."

"And she just gave the brooch to you?"

"She told me she'd been to see Davina, and Davina had shown her the piece. She told this woman that she had a plan to use it to try to prove some costume-jewelry necklace she had was part of the same set. It was convoluted, but Verna insisted Davina was scheming."

"How did she come to have the brooch?"

"She didn't say. But she said she wanted to return it to the museum, so I took it off her hands. Obviously."

"Yes, obviously. And you didn't go to Davina's apartment to speak to her?"

He shrugged. "I didn't see the point, to be honest. The woman's a con artist. There's nothing to be gained by engaging with her."

Grandmother turned the pin over in her hand. "Perhaps not. Well, it's a moot point now, as she's dead. And there's nothing to be gained by sharing this information with the police. It will only serve to further embroil us in this mess."

"Quite." He clasped his hands behind his back and adopted a somber expression.

She nodded and placed the brooch on her desk. She twisted a ring off her right ring finger, opened the small center drawer of her elegant writing desk, and dropped the ring into the tray. Then she handed the pin back to him.

"Very well done, Eugene. Hold on to this for now, but do keep it somewhere safe. There's no need to share this development with Lewis and his medical examiners. It's a private matter."

"Yes, Grandmother."

That suited him fine. He slipped the pin into his pocket.

23

As the ornate elevator juddered to a stop on the third floor, Bodhi touched Eliza's elbow. "Hang back," he whispered in her ear.

She showed no reaction, but when the highly polished doors opened with a groan, she stood motionless.

"This is us," Marvin said. "Mrs. Sullivan's office is at the end of the hall on the right."

"Lead the way," Eliza said with a smile.

She and Bodhi waited for Marvin and the chief to step out in the hallway first and then fell several paces behind the two.

"Marvin said Davina's cousin has a temper," Bodhi said in a low tone.

"Hmm."

"And I think Davina might have stolen a brooch from Cassie."

Eliza's hand flew to her mouth to stifle a gasp. Dexter turned around and shot them a questioning look. Just then, Marvin came to a stop in front of a door and knocked.

"Enter," an imperious voice called from within the room.

He opened the door and waved the three of them through it ahead of him.

Margot Rutherford Sullivan sat behind a Queen Anne-style writing desk that had complicated scrollwork and delicate-looking legs. She held a fountain pen in her right hand, and an incongruous, sleek laptop sat, closed, at her left elbow.

Sully stood behind her desk with his hands clasped behind him and a dazed expression on his face.

"Thank you for seeing our guests up, Mr. Washington. There's no need for you to stay." Margot's gracious tone masked the fact of the dismissal.

"Lewis, thank you for coming here to chat. It simply would have been disruptive for Eugene and me to come to the police station."

"No problem at all, Mrs. Sullivan. Besides, you know, I'm hosting that convention of police chiefs this weekend, so I'm just next door over at the lodge anyway."

Eliza raised an eyebrow at the obsequious *aw-shucks* tone.

Bodhi refrained from pointing out that they actually hadn't been just next door, that they had come from Davina's apartment in town, which, as it happened, was around the corner from the police station. It was better to let this vignette play out and get a sense of the dynamic between the doyenne of high society and the chief of police. Maybe he really *was* in her pocket.

Chief Dexter gestured toward Eliza and Bodhi. "This is Dr. Eliza Rollins. She's the medical examiner for St. Mary's Parish down in—"

"Ah, yes, Belle Rue, Louisiana. I've heard of you."

Bodhi was confident she'd never heard of Eliza before this morning—or yesterday evening, at the earliest. But her tone suggested she'd been following Eliza's career for decades.

"And that means you must be Dr. King."

She extended two limp fingers, one of which was weighed down with a large ring, and he shook them awkwardly. Her papery skin was warm and scented with a highly perfumed lotion.

"Pleased to meet you, Mrs. Sullivan."

With the pleasantries out of the way, Sully waved a hand at the seating arrangement. "Please, sit wherever you're comfortable."

Dexter plopped down into the nearest seat, a straight-backed chair covered in striped silk. Bodhi and Eliza, as if by unspoken agreement, headed for a plush settee situated between Margot Rutherford Sullivan's desk and a large bookcase.

Once they were seated, Margot took control. "Eugene tells me you have some news, Lewis. Presumably about Professor Jones' tragic death. So shocking that something like that would happen in our small town. Although, I'm told she resided on Pecan Boulevard. Not the best area." She made a *tsk* sound.

"That's right, Mrs. Sullivan. The neighborhood to the south of the police station, well, it can be a bit rough. Breaking and—"

Bodhi interrupted the chief and dispelled any notions of random crime or home invasions. "We've just come from the crime scene, ma'am. We're fairly certain Professor Jones knew her killer."

It was hard to tell whether Margot Sullivan was surprised by this news because her face was a smooth, impassive mask. She didn't twitch. Her eyes didn't widen. Her hand didn't flutter to her throat.

"Oh, my. Why do you say that?" she finally murmured.

"We're not at liberty to say—" Eliza began to recite the standard response to a request for information about an open murder investigation.

Dexter apparently was at liberty. He cast Eliza a warning look and explained, "There was no sign of forced entry, and nothing seemed to be missing. So the motive appears to be personal."

"Nothing was missing? You're sure?" Sully interjected.

Bodhi filed the weird question away in the back of his mind for later consideration.

"And, she was stabbed?" Margot asked.

"Yes, with a screwdriver from her archaeological tool kit."

Sully winced.

"She put up a fight, though," the chief continued on blithely. "Threw a knife at her attacker. Too bad she missed."

"She *threw* a knife? What an odd choice," Margot marveled.

"According to Dr. King, she was actually an accomplished ax thrower. Who knew?"

"Certainly not me. My word. I had no idea she had such a . . . violent streak. Now I'm even more convinced that our decision to end our relationship with her was the right one. And given that we *have* ended a relationship with Professor Jones, I'm curious why you think we'll be able to help. I doubt we have any information that you don't already know."

"I tried to tell him that on the phone, Grandmother."

Margot waved off her grandson. He fell silent.

Chief Dexter cleared his throat. "I just learned something from my forensic consultants that you should know. Dr. King?"

"When we were examining the coffin and the woman inside it this morning, Professor Jones unexpectedly turned up in the laboratory." He saw no reason to sugarcoat it.

Margot frowned. "Impossible. She was barred from the premises when we took her identification."

"Yes, but she talked her way onto the cleaning crew this morning and came in with them," Eliza said.

"Eugene, did you know anything about this?"

"Not until this very minute." Sully narrowed his eyes. "Wait. When I came down to the lab, there was a janitor in the room. Was that ...?"

"Yes, that was Davina. I guess you didn't recognize

her out of context," Bodhi said as neutrally as he could manage.

They both knew the truth: Eugene Sullivan never spared a glance for a member of the cleaning crew, so he'd had no chance of recognizing her.

"But you recognized her, didn't you?" Sully spat. "And you didn't alert me."

"Truthfully, I didn't think it was my place."

Margot didn't seem particularly scandalized by Bodhi and Eliza's failure to narc on Davina. She had another scapegoat in her sights. "This is unacceptable. How could she just sneak onto the cleaning crew? Get Marvin Washington back up here. And the janitorial supervisor."

Bodhi made a small noise in his throat. "Forgive me for butting in, but Mr. Washington told me the janitorial supervisor doesn't work weekends. He plans to speak to her on Monday."

Margot looked at him sharply. "You've spoken to Marvin?"

"Yes, when we came in. As I understand it, Professor Jones' cousin is a member of the cleaning crew and may have helped her gain access."

"What's this cousin's name? Eugene, get her up here. We need to get to the bottom of this breach."

"I believe that when Mr. Washington learned what

happened, he sent Verna, the cousin, home for the rest of the day. But I'm sure Chief Dexter would appreciate getting the cousin's address and telephone number, right?" Bodhi finished explaining, then turned to the police chief.

"We'll find it one way or the other. But if you could open your personnel files, I'd be much obliged."

Eliza shook her head. "Surely you don't think this Verna person killed Davina? Mere hours earlier, she'd *helped* her."

Margot lectured her, "You don't know much about human nature, do you, Dr. Rollins? Perhaps that's because you deal with the dead. I've had a lot of experience with the living, and it's safe to say that people react in unexpected ways all the time."

Bodhi seized the opening. "Yes. Speaking of unexpected reactions, it seems odd that you initially offered to pay for a forensic anthropologist or archaeologist to date the woman in the coffin that Davina found, then changed your mind. Why would the Rutherford Family Foundation refuse to sponsor the work needed to verify what's truly a remarkable cultural find?"

She didn't answer immediately. "Eugene tells me you believe that poor woman was murdered."

"She was hanged."

"Well, that's not the sort of history we work to bring to light."

"History is history. Surely you're not suggesting we can pick and choose what we preserve? If everyone did that, the historical record would be incomplete and inaccurate."

Margot smiled indulgently at Eliza. "My dear, do you really think that accuracy and completeness and all this ugliness is serving anyone? Wouldn't it be a better world if we chose to focus on the good, the inspiring, and the beautiful? I think so."

"That's an unusual position for the director of a historical organization to take."

"It may be, and not everyone agrees. For instance, the Isaiah Bell Archives takes a different, less optimistic view. They like to dredge up ugly episodes that would be better left alone."

The color was rising in Eliza's cheeks. Bodhi rested a hand on her arm as if to say it's not worth engaging with this woman. He needn't have worried, because Eliza didn't get the chance to engage.

Dexter launched into a long monologue about how grateful the department was for the foundation's assistance and patronage over the years. He vowed to close the matter of Davina's death without embarrassing either the Rutherford Family Foundation or the family itself.

He followed up with an apology for Bodhi and Eliza's behavior and assured Margot and Sully that he had no plans to open an investigation into the body that Davina had found. Despite the possibility that she'd been murdered, the woman would remain a Jane Doe.

The more he blathered on, the more agitated Bodhi grew. He had to move around to let out some energy. He stood and strolled over to the bookcase with his hands clasped behind his back to study the display of photographs and awards.

One large, silver-framed picture caught his eye. Chief Dexter, Margot, and Sully posed in front of a podium. Margot clutched a wooden plaque with a shiny bronze plate between her be-ringed fingers and beamed at the camera. It appeared to be a recent photograph.

Sully, who wasn't part of the conversation between his grandmother and Dexter, came over to stand beside Bodhi.

"Oh, that's Chief Dexter awarding my grandmother the Distinguished Citizen of the Year Award last year for all of her community service. And here's the award itself. We were all very proud of her." He pointed to the plaque, which was displayed on the shelf directly above the photograph.

Bodhi glanced up at the award but quickly returned his attention to the picture.

"Oh, that. I don't do it for the recognition. I do it to serve the community. It's part of the foundation's mission, after all," Margot interjected.

Then she stood, signaling that she'd had her fill of the chief's sycophantic fawning and that this interview was over.

"If there's anything at all that we can do to help, Chief Dexter, just call," Sully urged as he scampered toward the door. "I'll personally see that you get an address and telephone number for Professor Jones' cousin before you leave."

Sully opened the door with a theatrical gesture, and Eliza paused just inside the threshold. "Oh, I think one question slipped the chief's mind. Where were you between the hours of eleven and one today?"

"I beg your pardon. Are you asking me for an alibi?" Sully's eyes flitted to Margot.

"Now, Sully, of course not." Dexter frowned.

Eliza smiled her sweetest smile. "We'd like to rule you and your grandmother out."

"Rule me out," Margot said heartily. "My dear, do I

strike you as someone who would plunge a screwdriver into someone's—what was it—thigh?"

"Looks can be deceiving, Mrs. Sullivan. After all, Professor Jones didn't strike you as the sort of person who would wield an ax, did she?"

"You don't need to answer these questions, either of you. In fact, I'm advising you not to," Chief Dexter said, red-faced. He stormed out of the office, leaving Bodhi and Eliza no choice but to follow.

24

Dexter was still apoplectic when he arranged for Officer Rey to drive Bodhi and Eliza back to the lodge. He stayed behind with Officer Kincaid to speak to Marvin Washington and get an address for Davina's cousin. They settled into the back seat and waited until their short journey from the museum back to the lodge was underway to begin speaking. Thanks to the cage and the bulletproof glass separating the front and back seats and the road noise, the driver wouldn't be able to make out much, if any, of their conversation.

"I guess we hit a nerve when we asked Sully and Mrs. Sullivan if they could account for their whereabouts, huh?" Eliza said, a bit sheepish.

"I think you would've gotten away with it if you'd

stopped with Sully. But asking Margot Sullivan for an alibi was a bridge too far."

She laughed, but her eyes had a faraway look. She was thinking about something. He waited.

After a moment, she said, "Everyone seems pretty eager to pin Davina's death on her cousin."

"According to Marvin, they did have an argument. There's motive. And because he sent her home early, she could have gone to Davina's apartment. That's opportunity."

"And the means was right there in Davina's basket of tools. She does satisfy all three tentpoles. Still ..."

"I'm not saying she's our killer. I'm just saying it makes sense for Dexter to start with her. She's a strong suspect."

"Only if you believe Davina's death is unrelated to her discovery of Cassie and the coffin."

"You think it's related?"

"I don't know. But it's awfully convenient timing for bad blood between Davina and Verna to boil over, don't you think?"

He did think. But he also knew firsthand that family ties landed a large proportion of people in the morgue. She knew so, too.

"Well, seeing as how we're on Dexter's naughty list,

we're not going to get a chance to talk to Verna anyway, so you and I should focus elsewhere."

"Micah, you mean?"

He lowered his voice. "Yes. We should call him when we get back and ask him about his conversation with Davina."

A shadow of trouble flitted across her face, and she shifted her gaze toward the front of the squad car. Officer Rey seemed to be focused on the squawking coming from the dispatch radio. She leaned closer anyway.

"I think it's a good idea. I noticed in the activity log that she texted Micah as well, right after she ended the call with him. There was a paperclip icon next to the text message entry."

"So she sent him a file or a photograph or something?"

"It looks like. We need to get to him before Clive finishes reviewing the phone and tells Dexter about it."

"I'm sure Bette and Fred will understand if we beg off tonight's social activities in light of a murder investigation. Right?"

Eliza's gaze was fixed on a distant point along the winding drive as they approached the lodge, and she didn't respond.

"Eliza?" he prompted.

"Sorry." She continued to stare out the window "I'm not so sure they will."

"What do you mean?"

She pointed toward the entrance of the lodge. "Mom and Dad look pissed."

He leaned across the seat and followed her finger. A fuming Fred and a stormy-faced Bette stood in identical poses at the base of the stairs to the main entrance. Both struck wide-hipped stances with their fists on their hips.

Officer Rey brought the car to a stop, parked, and came around to Eliza's side of the back seat to let them out. He glanced at the glowering figures standing in front of the stairs. "You two have one heck of a welcoming committee waiting for you."

"If you only knew," Eliza muttered under her breath as Rey held the door open for her. After she climbed out, she turned back and smirked at Bodhi. "I'm just going to have to tell Fred that you're a bad influence on me. "

"Wha -?" But she was already halfway to the stairs, calling a goodbye to the police officer over her shoulder.

Bodhi hauled himself off the seat. "Thanks for the lift, Officer Rey."

"My pleasure. If you don't mind a piece of advice?"

Bodhi paused beside the car. "I'll take all the help I can get."

Rey nodded sagely. "I find that when I get in the doghouse with my girlfriend, I just have to remind her that law enforcement is a different world, and she can't really understand all the things I go through. Now you all are medical examiners. Your significant others, they've just gotta understand that when there's a murder investigation, a weekend getaway at some fancy resort has to take a back seat. That's just the way it goes. "

Bodhi grinned wryly. "Thanks for the tip, but those two people standing there looking like thunderclouds? They're both the police chiefs of their towns. They're here for Chief Dexter's conference. So I don't think the 'you don't understand law enforcement' argument is going to carry much weight."

"Oh yeah, you're screwed. It's been nice knowing you." He shook Bodhi's hand gravely.

Bodhi squared his shoulders and walked toward the entrance. By the time he reached Bette's side, Fred and Eliza were halfway up the steps.

"Hi. You look upset."

"Do I? That's probably because I am. I got a call from Chief Dexter."

He studied the tightness in her jaw and the clench of her teeth, then chose his words with care. "I assume he called to tell you that he asked Eliza and me to help out with a murder investigation?"

At the mention of the murder, her expression slackened. "I was sorry to hear about Professor Jones. It sounds like it was..."

"Horrific."

Her eyes softened with concern. "Do you want to talk about it?"

He did. But he also knew she had something she wanted to get off her chest. And it was always better to experience your emotions and then let them go than to dwell on them.

"I do. But first, I want to talk about whatever's got you so angry."

She dragged her hands through her silvery hair, then massaged her temples, rubbing small circles with two fingers on both sides.

After a long moment, she said, "Did you accuse the most prominent citizen of this postage-stamp town of murder?"

"That's a bit of an exaggeration. We went to Davina's apartment at Chief Dexter's request, remember? The town's coroner is away on vacation. So Eliza and I did the chief a favor." He trailed off. He took a long centering breath. "I sound defensive, don't I?"

"You do."

"Let's start again. But can we do this inside?—it's kind of chilly out here."

She pursed her lips. "Sure."

He wondered whether it was going to be equally chilly inside, given her mood. But as they mounted the stairs, she slipped her hand inside his.

They found a small wrought-iron table in the hallway in a quiet corner of the lobby's coffee bar and ordered hot drinks from a passing waiter.

Bodhi inhaled the ginger-lemon scent of his tisane and warmed his hands on the mug while Bette stirred oat milk into her coffee. After she tasted it and nodded her approval, he dove back into his story.

"We realized when we were at the crime scene that we'd have to tell Chief Dexter about Davina coming to the museum this morning. He needs to have an accurate account of her movements in her final hours."

"That was the right decision."

"I think so, too. But it ticked him off." She opened her mouth as if to defend the chief, but he held up a hand. "Let me finish. So he was already angry when Eliza asked Eugene Sullivan and Mrs. Sullivan if they could account for their whereabouts at the time of Davina's murder. That's when he blew up."

Her eyes went wide. "And neither of you thought that was impolitic?"

It was his turn to massage his temples. "I'm a forensic pathologist. Most of the people I work with are dead, Bette. I'm not in the habit of running my theories and ideas through a filter to determine whether they're impolitic. I imagine the same's true for Eliza."

She snorted, indignant and incensed. "You've been involved in how many high-profile, political scandals and sensitive investigations? You and your little girlfriend should know better than to stomp around like gorillas in a small town that's not your own."

He sipped his tea. She looked down at her coffee mug but didn't pick it up. After a moment, she said, "You don't have anything to say in response to that?" She kept her eyes on the mug.

"Is this about Chief Dexter's anger? Or is it about something else?"

She shook her head and laughed huskily, her eyes still downcast. "I'm not jealous of the time you're spending with Eliza if that's what you're driving at. I shouldn't have called her your girlfriend, though. That was childish. I chose my words poorly because I'm angry. Your behavior in this investigation reflects on *me*."

"Bette—"

"No, let me finish. Lewis Dexter won't hesitate to trash my reputation. Not for a moment. That matters to me. I've worked hard. To get where I've got—especially as a woman— I've had to be tactful and circumspect. I can't stand by while you and some medical examiner from Louisiana undo all my efforts. And while I don't speak for Fred, you're damaging his standing among our peers, too."

"Bette, I'm sorry. I never meant to put you in a bad spot. I'm genuinely sorry."

When she raised her head and looked at him, unshed tears glistened in her eyes. "Thank you. Will you promise me you'll remove yourself from Davina Jones' murder investigation and the investigation into Cassie in the coffin? Please?"

Bodhi inhaled, paused, then exhaled deeply. He placed his hand over hers, squeezed gently, and then said, "No."

25

Fred paced around the hotel room in fast, angry circles. Watching him made Eliza dizzy. As he started another circuit by the bathroom, she patted the couch cushion to the left of where she sat.

"Sit down so we can talk. I feel like I'm on the teacup ride at Christmas at Acadian Village." She smiled.

He paused mid-step. "Is this a joke to you?"

"What? No."

"Then why bring up Noel Acadian?"

She blinked at him. "Because we were just there a few weeks ago over the holidays, and the teacups made me nauseous. Remember?"

"Eliza, I'm trying to have a serious conversation with you. I'm concerned."

"I can see that. I can also see that you're all worked up. It would be a lot easier to talk if you would just sit down."

He made a low strangled sound of frustration but, after a moment, joined her on the couch.

"Thank you."

"I guess I *am* a little agitated," he conceded. "But these things you're doing, they're not only foolish, they're dangerous."

"What I'm doing is no more dangerous than what I do every day back home. Today I examined a dead body and was called to a murder scene. That's my job."

He was silent for a long, long time. So long, in fact, that she thought he wasn't going to respond. He twisted his hands together, wringing them over and over.

Finally, he said, "This may be what you do every day, but you don't do it like this. You don't do it with Bodhi King."

She stiffened. "That's what this is really about, right? You don't like Bodhi."

"No, you're wrong. I don't like Bodhi's methods. What he's doing—what you're doing with him— isn't just endangering you, it's endangering all the progress you've made."

She opened her mouth to protest, but he continued. "Now don't get all het up at me. I'm not saying he's not good at what he does. Far as I can tell, he's a brilliant forensic pathologist. Maybe even as good as you, but that doesn't mean he's good *for* you. And I'm concerned about you."

She had to hold back a giggle. When she told Bodhi she was going to say he was a bad influence on her, she'd been joking. But Fred apparently believed it.

"I'm sorry you're worried. I really am. And if Bodhi and I have put you in a bad spot with Chief Dexter and the rest of the police chiefs, I'm sorry for that, too."

He pulled a face as if to say she should know him better than that. But the fact was, he was a law enforcement officer, and they did tend toward the straight and narrow.

"I appreciate that. And I'm not trying to be paternalistic. Honest. But, I'm going to ask you to let all of this go—the woman in the iron coffin, Davina Jones' murder, all of it—for me. Can you do that?"

She was quiet for a long, long, long time. Even longer than his earlier silence. And she spent that time searching her heart to see if she could do what he asked. And she took no pleasure when she softly said, "No. I'm sorry, I can't."

He gaped at her in wounded surprise and was about to open his mouth when three firm raps sounded on their door.

Tap, tap, tap.

"I'll get it!" She hopped up and flung open the door to reveal a tight-lipped Bette and a resigned Bodhi standing in the hall. Bodhi was a half-step behind Bette. *Sorry,* he mouthed.

"Yes?" she asked, shaking off the feeling that she was a high school kid who'd just been busted by her parents. Ironic, because that wasn't a scenario she'd experienced as an actual high school student.

"We apparently need something that's on Eliza's phone," Bette explained to Fred, adult-to-adult, as she and Bodhi crossed the threshold into the room.

26

Sully slumped a bit, rounding his shoulders and casting his gaze on the ground while he waited for Dexter. It wouldn't do for anyone to recognize him.

He was so intent on staring at the patch of earth under his feet that he didn't hear the police chief approaching the gazebo from the lodge.

"Hiya, Sully," Dexter boomed.

He jumped at least a foot off the ground and landed with his legs splayed. "Honestly."

Dexter pounded him on the back. "Sorry. So, what can I do for you?"

He brushed invisible lint off his jacket, then cleared his throat. "Well, as I mentioned on the phone, this is a sensitive matter."

"Right. That's why we're meeting in person. And we're meeting here because I need to get back inside before we sit down for dinner. So ..."

"Yes, sorry. I'll get right to it. There's a necklace in Davina Jones' apartment. I need it. It's a gold chain with a large gold pendant with intricate filigree work. A sizable facet-cut garnet is set in the middle of the pendant. It looks very similar to this." He pulled the brooch from his pocket and passed it to Dexter.

Dexter examined it for a long moment, poking his tongue into the side of his cheek, then handed it back. "Did she steal this necklace from the museum or something?"

"Perhaps, in a roundabout way."

"You'll have to be a bit less cryptic and a bit more forthcoming if you want me to remove jewelry from a murder scene."

"That's fair, I suppose. You're aware that the Rutherford Trust documents specify that only female descendants of Louisa Anne Rutherford can serve as trustees and take as beneficiaries?"

"How could I not be? You've been harping on about it for years."

He bristled. "Right. Well, one way to establish lineage is through ownership of one of three pieces of jewelry. This brooch is one, and the necklace that

Davina Jones somehow had in her possession when she died *may* be another one."

"What's the third?"

Sully pretended not to hear the question. "It's imperative that I have the opportunity to examine that necklace to determine its provenance. Your consultants and officers can't know. And Grandmother certainly can't know."

Dexter hid a grin. "Sully, you sly dog. What are you up to? Okay, I'll see what I can do."

They shook hands and were about to go their separate directions when a town car ferrying Eliza Rollins, Bodhi King, and another man and woman bumped past on the gravel road.

"Wonder where they're off to?" Sully mused.

The police chief narrowed his eyes. "So do I."

27

Micah stared into the depths of his masala chai. "She's really dead?" His voice was raw, shaky. "I just talked to her a few hours ago."

Bodhi met Eliza's eyes over Micah's bent head. She pursed her lips in thought, and then placed a hand on the grief-dazed man's arm and spoke to him in a soft voice. Bodhi couldn't make out her words over the acoustic rock music piped through the restaurant's sound system.

Whatever she said must have been a balm to the librarian, though. He raised his head and cupped his hands around his oversized mug. He looked at the far wall for a long moment, seemingly focused on an abstract piece of art titled "Tempest."

Bodhi followed his gaze. The paint-drizzled canvas evoked Jackson Pollock. Bodhi looked more closely and amended his opinion: the technique was actually closer to the work of Janet Sobel—the lesser-known, self-taught Ukrainian-American artist who influenced Pollock's style.

Focus.

He returned his attention to Micah, who filled his lungs with air, straightened his spine, and turned to look first at Eliza and then at Bodhi. "I'll tell you everything I know. There's no chance the police will investigate thoroughly, not after what Davina told me."

They both leaned across the table toward him. From the next table over, Bette and Fred both leaned forward, too. They would not be dissuaded from chaperoning, but after intense negotiating, they'd agreed to give Eliza and Bodhi some space to talk to the last person who spoke to Davina.

"What did she say?"

"She told me about the find first—the coffin and, uh, Cassie. Then she said she overhead the Sullivans plotting to smear her reputation so nobody would believe her if she went public about Cassie."

"When?" Bodhi asked.

"When what?"

"When did she hear this conversation?"

"Today. I think after she left the two of you in the lab, she might have . . . well . . . eavesdropped on Mrs. Sullivan and Sully."

"Why didn't she tell us? She could have texted or called you." Eliza spoke out of the side of her mouth and directed her comment to Bodhi.

But Micah answered. "I'm sure she would've. But she asked me to look into some things for her first. Knowing Davina, she would have wanted to come to you with an answer, or at least an idea, and not just a problem."

"What things?"

"She wanted to know if there were any reports of white women—possibly teachers from up north—being threatened or harassed."

"Or lynched?"

"That too," Micah conceded.

"And?"

"I haven't found anything yet, but I'll need more time. Like I told her, the archives aren't fully indexed."

"Anything else?"

"She texted me a picture of a pin—technically, I think it's a brooch."

The brooch again.

"Did she say why the piece was important?" Bodhi

would've leaned further across the table, but he would've been in Micah's lap if he'd done so.

"Well, no. But she didn't need to. It was."

Micah looked at them as if this riddle explained everything.

Eliza turned to Bodhi. "Is this some kind of a thingy ...?"

"Zen koan?" Bette chimed in from her table. "Sure sounds like one."

Eliza chortled.

Bodhi waited until their laughter died down, then he said, "Please, go on."

He couldn't pretend that he wasn't encouraged by their shared moment. He was.

Micah explained, "All her life, Davina's granny had told her that she was related to a civil rights leader who'd lived during Reconstruction. She was convinced it was Isaiah Matthew Bell. That's how we met—she used to spend hours in the archives looking for a connection to Isaiah. But she never found one. Anyway, when her grandmother died, Davina's mom inherited the necklace. It was supposed to prove her ancestry or something. Davina's mom was diagnosed with stage four brain cancer last year. She went fast."

"How sad," Eliza murmured.

It was sad, but Bodhi didn't yet see how this was

tied to the brooch.

Breathing in, I am patient. Breathing out, I listen.

Micah went on, "The necklace went to Davina after her mom passed. After that, she was obsessed with tracing it back to Isaiah Bell. I tried to help her, but I couldn't find a thing about that necklace. Honestly? I think part of the reason she submitted the grant application to excavate the Jonah Bell Farm was because she hoped she'd find a connection there."

"Did she?" Eliza asked.

"A day ago, I would have told you no. But, now ... The brooch is an important piece of the puzzle. I can't say for sure *what* significance it has. Not yet. But, yeah, I *can* say it's important."

"Why do you say that?" Eliza wanted to know.

"Because Davina has a necklace just like that brooch. I mean, it's identical."

"You're sure? Same filigree, same stone, same everything?" Bodhi pressed.

"Positive. I mean, I only saw a cell phone picture of the pin. But it was clear and a closeup. And I must've seen Davina's necklace a thousand times. They were identical. One was turned into a pendant. And one was turned into a brooch or pin. But the stones are the same. And the scrollwork pattern is the same. They were obviously made by the same craftsperson."

Micah nodded. He was sure.

"Where did she get that brooch?" Fred asked, forgetting the no-talking zone in his eagerness to hear the answer.

"I'm pretty sure she removed it from Cassie's body. When we went back to the museum to talk to the Sullivans, Marvin Washington mentioned that Margot had been in the lab this morning, staring through the coffin's glass window at a brooch fastened to the neck of Cassie's blouse."

"Hang on. This jewelry belonged to the dead woman? And Davina took it?" Bette asked.

"I think so." Bodhi turned to Eliza. "Did you happen to notice it when we were looking at her through the window?"

She shook her head. "No. And we should have seen it when we were trying to unbutton Cassie's collar without destroying the fabric. There was no brooch. I'm sure."

Micah chuckled. "Did Davina have access to the garment? Even for a few seconds?"

"Sure, probably. When we were easing the coffin lid off, she could have reached in—or right after. But we would've seen her," Bodhi said.

"No, you wouldn't have."

All four of them stared at Micah, waiting.

"She put herself through college by performing as a magician. Sleight of hand was her specialty."

"Sonofa ..."

Eliza shot Fred a look, and he trailed off.

"So, the brooch and the necklace are a matched set?" Bodhi mused.

"They must be."

"How do they prove Davina's a descendant of Matthew Bell if half the set was buried with an unidentified white woman?" Bodhi shook his head.

"I can't see a link," Micah agreed. "Unless ...."

"Unless?"

"This is just a wild-eyed guess, okay? It's not even a theory." He looked around to make sure everyone understood before continuing. "The Rutherford Family Foundation was established by a trust agreement. I know, because the land that the Bell farm sits on was included in the original grant."

"Okay."

"The foundation is a private charitable trust. Some, but not all, of its organizational documents were filed publicly. And it was established in 1874, so some of them have probably been lost or destroyed."

"Got it, go on," Bodhi prompted.

"The original grantor was Louisa Anne Rutherford. Her husband predeceased her and left her a fortune. They had daughters, but no sons, so the family fortune was in the hands of the Rutherford women. Louisa decided it should stay that way."

"Meaning?"

"Meaning the foundation is controlled by female descendants of Louisa Rutherford, and female descendants only."

"What happens when there are none?"

"It dissolves. That's the rumor, at least. There's been lots of talk because Sully is the end of the line, and you may have noticed he's a dude."

"Huh."

"There's another rumor, too. That there's another Rutherford heir lurking around out there, and she's going to step forward when Margot passes away."

The pieces started to click into place. "You think this dead woman was a Rutherford?"

"It's possible. And DNA analysis would confirm it, right?"

"Yes," Bodhi told him.

"So that's why the Sullivans are opposed to it? They don't want to confirm that another branch of the family died out?" Bette hypothesized.

"It fits."

"It might. But it doesn't explain Davina's necklace."

"And it doesn't give Verna a motive to kill her,"

Eliza added.

"The police suspect Verna?" Micah's eyes widened.

"Yes. She was angry with Davina, and she was sent home from work early, so the timing of the murder works. Personally, I think Dexter is trying to frame her to keep the Sullivans happy," Eliza mused.

Micah interjected, "Maybe, but maybe not. Verna's a nasty piece of work, and there was bad blood between her and Davina. In fact, I was kind of surprised when Davina said she'd helped her out. I'm guessing Davina had to pay her."

"Do you know why they didn't get along?"

"Actually, that necklace of Davina's was the start of all their trouble. Davina's grandmother left it to Davina's mom rather than Verna's. Now those two, the moms, weren't sisters. They were some kind of distant cousins themselves. I don't know how the will worked, but Verna seemed to think she should have gotten the necklace. When she didn't . . . it got ugly."

"We need to get our hands on Davina's necklace if we can," Bodhi said.

"The crime scene is sealed. And there's no way that Dexter's gonna let us go back there," Eliza countered.

"Not us, but maybe someone else?" He looked at Fred and Bette.

"No," they said in unison.

28

Sunday morning

Eliza woke before the birds. She'd slept poorly, and continuing to toss and turn would only disturb Fred's slumber, too. So she slipped from the bed, wrapped herself in the lodge-provided thick terry robe, and padded silently into the bathroom.

She couldn't get Davina Jones out of her mind. Cassie's brooch and its possible connection to Davina's necklace gnawed at her. She was sure if she could get her hands on that necklace, it would answer some of her questions about the two murders. She could feel it.

But Dexter had unequivocally kicked them off the case, Fred was refusing to help, and Bodhi could not or would not tell a lie. So that left only one choice: it was up to her.

She splashed water on her face, brushed her teeth, and slipped into the most appropriate cat burglar clothing she could unearth from her suitcase in the dark bedroom. Black yoga pants and a long-sleeved gray t-shirt emblazoned with the logo of a 10K race sponsor. A black fleece jacket over top. She tiptoed out into the hallway in her socks, eased the door shut, and then put on her running shoes and laced them up. Then she raced down the stairs before she could second guess her plan.

As she hurried through the lobby, Jason called to her. "Good morning, Dr. Rollins, do you need a driver?"

She gestured toward her clothes. "Thanks, but I'm good. Just going for a hike."

She couldn't risk involving Jason in her planned crime.

"Looks like a nice morning for it!" He gave her a cheerful goodbye wave.

She pushed open the door, filled her lungs with the crisp air, and headed toward the hiking path. As soon as she was out of view of the lodge, she stopped under a gazebo, pulled up a ride-sharing app, and requested a trip to 1400 Pecan Boulevard.

She jogged out to the entrance to wait for Ruthie V., the driver, while the sky gradually lightened, and morning dawned.

A bright yellow VW bug crested the hill, turned on its flashers, and pulled to the side of the road. She hopped in and greeted the driver. She hoped Ruthie wouldn't be the chatty type because she needed to use the drive to settle her nerves.

"Morning, sunshine!" Ruthie trilled. "Do you mind if I listen to the end of this opera on our trip into town?"

"Have at it."

"Lovely." She turned up the volume on her car stereo. "It's Act 3, the assassin is just about to stab Gilda. I've got my Kleenex at the ready." She pointed to a travel pack of tissues on her passenger seat."

"A Verdi fan, huh?"

"*Rigoletto's* my favorite opera," the driver confirmed. "So tragic."

Eliza leaned her head back against the headrest and closed her eyes as Ruthie executed a U-turn and began the descent down the mountain. All Verdi operas were tragic, weren't they? Between the murders and the suicides, a night at the opera was pretty much just like a day in the morgue. She could only hope the soundtrack wasn't an omen for the day ahead.

S neaking into Davina's apartment was easier than it should have been. Later, she'd wonder if that had been by design.

She'd been prepared to talk her way past Officer Rey or his replacement, but when she exited the VW bug, she didn't see a police cruiser parked in the lot. She checked the fire door. No uniformed officer posted.

The absence of law enforcement outside the apartment actually ratcheted up the difficulty level. Now she needed to find some other way in. She walked around to the front of the building and studied the names affixed alongside the rows of buzzers in an effort to divine which resident might be inclined to buzz in a stranger at six o'clock in the morning on a Sunday.

She was trying to decide between Chang, Stanley, and Maxwell, Ethel, when the elevator bell dinged inside, then the sound of howling and barking filled the lobby. She stood to the side as a harried dog walker wearing a vest emblazoned with the name

'Pawsitively Purrfect Pet Care' careened toward the door amid a tangle of leashes. Eliza counted a Pomeranian, a Shepard of some kind, a beagle mix, and at least two retrievers in the dervish of fur and paws that pounded through the door.

"Here, let me hold that for you," she offered, grabbing the door as the dog walker paused on the threshold to untangle a leash from around his ankle.

"Thanks. Have a good one," he called as he was yanked toward the park across the road by his cadre of canines.

She edged through the door and hurried to the elevator bank. She pressed the up button, then thought better of it and headed for the stairwell instead.

Davina's apartment door was ajar. The crime scene tape still stretched across the doorway, but it sagged and drooped as if it were tired. She ducked under.

"Clive?"

Her voice echoed in the stillness of the apartment, but no answer sounded. She walked through the kitchen and poked her head into the hall bathroom.

"Hello?"

The room was empty.

If nobody's here, then why is the front door ajar? Her brain demanded an answer, but she didn't have one.

She continued toward the rear of the apartment, ill at ease and jumpy. Maybe Clive or some other forensic technician had just left on a coffee run. Or Detective Valtri had needed a hand with something. There were lots of possibilities, but none of them gave her much comfort. The best thing to do was just find the necklace and get out of the apartment. She quickened her pace.

When she reached the door to Davina's bedroom, she pushed it open with her elbow, then stood in the doorway and surveyed the space. The room was feminine and bright, and–even after having been processed by the forensic team—it retained an organized tidiness.

Good. The orderliness should make it easy to find where Davina kept her jewelry.

She scanned the room, hoping to spot a jewelry box sitting atop the dresser or vanity. No such luck. She pursed her lips and thought. She kept her jewelry, such as it was, in a wall-mounted jewelry armoire hung in her oversized closet.

It seemed unlikely that an apartment this size would feature a walk-in closet, but she stepped into the room and slowly turned in a full circle to check. Nope. But on the east wall, across from the bed, a pair of paneled bifold doors was set into the wall.

She pulled her jacket cuffs down over her hands and pushed the doors open, cursing herself for failing to bring along a package of forensic gloves. The shallow closet was as well organized as the rest of the apartment. Scarves, blouses, and dresses hung on the left side. Slacks, pantsuits, and jackets were on the right. Shoes were lined up on wire racks that sat on the floor. She looked up.

Above the clothes rod, a white wire shelf held a rectangular rosewood box, roughly the dimensions of a ream of paper. She reached it easily but had to grip it with her fingers for fear of dropping it. She made a note to wipe her prints from the surface before she left.

She carried the box to Davina's queen bed and perched on the edge of the bed, balancing the treasure box across her knees. She raised the hinged lid carefully to reveal a deep blue velvet tray with at least a dozen individual compartments. Earrings and rings were nestled in the various tiny compartments. With two fingers, she lifted the velvet tray out of the box and placed it on the bed. A second tray lay beneath the first, divided into two long, skinny compartments. One held bracelets. The other, necklaces.

Bingo.

There it was. Between a small string of pearls and

a chunky turquoise choker. The same filigree pattern as the brooch Bodhi had shown her. The same garnet stone. The only difference to her eye was that this piece was strung on a delicate chain rather than set with a pin closure. Her hands shook with anticipation as she plucked it from the tray. She rubbed a finger over the polished metal.

Davina had taken good care of the necklace. It was hard to believe it was the same age as the tarnished brooch that she'd removed from Cassie's blouse.

A floorboard creaked in the hall.

Eliza froze. She listened hard for another sound from the hallway, which was a challenge because her heart was drumming against her ribs. The floor did not creak, but she thought she heard breathing.

With fingers that now trembled not from excitement, but from fear, she fastened the necklace around her neck and placed the pendant against her skin, under her shirt. Then she returned the top tray to the box and glided across the room, ninja-like, to place the box in the closet.

She winced and pulled the closet doors shut, worried that they would squeal in their tracks. But they closed soundlessly, and she exhaled, relieved.

With the box back in place and the necklace hidden beneath her shirt and jacket, she cleared her throat and called, "Clive? Is that you? It's me—Eliza Rollins."

She walked toward the door and glanced up the hallway but saw no one. Frowning, she stepped out into the hall. As she strode toward the kitchen, she sensed movement on her periphery. She turned and saw the flat side of a trowel slicing through the air, headed directly toward her temple.

No.

It was part instinct, part instantaneous appraisal of her best-case scenario that made her turn *toward* the blow rather than twist away. As the heavy metal struck her solidly in the forehead, her last cogent thought was 'good.' Better to be smacked in the brow than to absorb a blow at the base of her skull—or even worse, her temple.

She swayed on her feet for a woozy moment, then crumpled to the floor. She'd have a monstrous headache when she woke up. But at least she had a chance of waking up rather than dying of a brain hemorrhage. Her hand fluttered toward her neck, then fell limply by her side. The trowel clattered to the wood beside her.

odhi and Bette lazed in bed, reading the newspaper on their phones, drinking tea and coffee, and watching through the floor-to-ceiling window as the sun came up over the mountains. It was quiet and cozy and it was good.

Bodhi turned his full attention to this moment. The song of the birds chirping outside. The warmth of Bette's long leg stretched out over his. The gingery tang of his tea and the rich scent of her coffee. There was nothing but the moment.

In a few hours, she'd be sitting in a conference room listening to some speaker talk about bulletproof glass or community policing or diversity in hiring, and her absence would be a tangible thing. Until then, he pushed aside all thoughts of Davina, Cassie, Dexter, the Rutherford Family—all of it. Until then, he would be here. Present and mindful.

Bodhi assumed the Sullivans would assert possession of both the casket and its occupant despite—or, maybe, because of—their desire to conceal the discovery of both. But he had the entire afternoon to make other arrangements. As soon as Bette's conference programming resumed, he'd call the Smithsonian.

Focus on the now, he reminded himself. Neither the past nor the future was real. This moment was the only moment.

He propped himself up on his elbow and traced a faint smile line on Bette's cheek with his finger. In response to his touch, she smiled, and the line deepened. She lifted her head from her pillow, arching her back to meet him, and—

Bang, bang, bang.

An insistent knock on the door intruded.

They jumped out of bed.

"Who is it?" Bette called.

"It's Fred. Sorry to bother you, but it's urgent." His frantic voice cracked.

Bodhi hurried over and unlatched the brass chain

lock, letting the lock swing down and sway against the door while he pulled the door open.

Fred stood in the doorway, his hands hanging loosely at his sides, and blinked as he scanned the room. "Have you seen Eliza?"

"No, we've been in the room all morning."

Bette came around the side of the bed, tightening her robe over the light pajamas she wore. That's when Bodhi realized he was shirtless, clad only in a pair of sweatpants. He scanned the room and found his shirt draped over a chair. He pulled it on over his head and smoothed down his unruly hair.

Fred dropped his face into his big hands, and his shoulders shook. "She's gone—Eliza's gone."

"What do you mean, gone?"

"Pretty much what it sounds like. I woke up and she wasn't there."

"Maybe she got up early and decided to take a walk?" Bette suggested.

"Or she went for a hike, or made an appointment at the spa," Bodhi chimed in.

"I checked everywhere. She did tell the valet that she was taking a hike—before the sun had even come up. I tracked her as far as the gazebo at the entrance to the loop trail. She never set foot on the trail. Her shoe prints cut through the front lawn and out to the road. Someone picked her up."

Bodhi shook his head slowly. "I'm as mystified as you are. I haven't talked to Eliza since we were all at the restaurant meeting with Micah Birch. So I'm sorry, but I couldn't begin to tell you where she might be."

Even as he said the words, he realized where Eliza was. If Eliza hadn't asked Jason to drive her wherever she was going, it was because she didn't want to make him complicit in something untoward. And, with that understanding, he knew what unsavory errand would propel Eliza out of bed under cover of darkness.

"What?" Bette studied his expression with a bright-eyed, penetrative look.

Incongruously, it reminded him of Eliza Doolittle, the macaw, when she tilted her head and stared at him sharp-eyed as if she were reading his soul.

He considered his options. If Eliza was where he thought she was, doing what he thought she was doing, Bette and Fred would push to tell Dexter. And he didn't want to do that.

But Fred's worry was so alive it was a separate entity, a frenzied mass of nerves. Bodhi had the ability to soothe Fred's beast. Did he have a duty to?

"Bodhi."

He waited, but that was all Bette said. Just his

name. Somehow, it was a full sentence. A short story. A three-act play.

"She didn't tell me where she was going, or what her plans were. I need you to hear that first, Fred. That's the truth."

Fred ground his teeth and nodded.

"If I were Eliza, and I left the property without telling anyone, it would be so that I could go back to Davina's apartment and poke around to see if I could find the necklace Micah told us about last night."

Fred gaped at him. "You're telling me she went back to an active crime scene—a crime scene she's been barred from, mind you—with the intent of breaking and entering and stealing evidence?"

While that wasn't the gloss he'd put on it, Bodhi didn't see the benefit of arguing the finer points with a distraught man. "I think she thinks it's an important piece to the puzzle of Davina's death, and possibly Cassie's identity. And I think she's right."

Fred shook his head, dismissing the idea—or maybe dismissing Bodhi himself. It was hard to tell. He turned to Bette.

"I can't call Lewis Dexter about this. On the off-chance she's *not* out breaking the law, I don't want to get him all stirred up needlessly. Will you come with me to check out the apartment?"

She didn't hesitate. "Of course. Give me a minute to put some clothes on."

She grabbed her handgun from the bedside table and stuffed it into the pocket of her robe. Then she scooped up her weekend bag and hurried into the bathroom. Bodhi watched Fred try to wrestle his incandescent worry into submission.

"She's going to be okay. You know, she's tougher than she looks."

"I know her better than you do. And, you're right, she's tougher than she looks. She's all but conquered her panic attacks. She's strong and smart . . . And entirely human. Someone murdered Davina Jones less than twenty-four hours ago, and I'll bet she was strong and smart, too."

He didn't have an answer for that. Luckily, Bette emerged from the bathroom, dressed and ready to roll, so he didn't have to come up with one.

"You should stay here," Bette told him. "I'm sure you're worried about Eliza, too. But if we need to involve Lewis Dexter, it'll be a lot cleaner if you aren't in the picture. No offense."

"None taken. Jason drove us there yesterday; he'll know the address. Go, get Eliza, and bring her back safe and sound."

Bette kissed his cheek absently before making a

'let's go' gesture with her hand to Fred and yanking open the door.

He listened until their footsteps faded in the hallway. Then he grabbed his cell phone to make a call.

He had a little breaking and entering of his own to do while they were busy at Davina's apartment.

30

Eliza regained consciousness in the dark and smelled blood. But not just blood. The familiar coppery scent intermingled with another smell. Tangy earth and rust and . . . this would be a whole lot easier if she could see.

She raised herself onto her elbows and promptly smacked her already-pounding forehead against something hard and unyielding. The sensation stole her breath, and she collapsed onto her back. After a long, nauseous moment, she touched her brow gingerly. The brush of her fingertips sent a fresh jolt of agony careening through her central nervous system, radiating out from her brain to her body. She sucked in a breath and pulled back her hand. It was sticky—confirmation that the blood she smelled was her own.

Groggily, from the center of a miasma of pain and misery, she pulled the memory of the trowel swinging through the air. She saw the trajectory, on a course with her vulnerable temple, and remembered turning toward it to protect her brain.

She rewound further. Returning Davina's jewelry box to the closet shelf. Fastening the necklace around her neck. She patted her breastbone and felt the reassuring bump of metal and gemstone under her shirt.

Even further. A creaking floorboard. She'd thought one of the police officers or crime scene technicians had returned to the apartment. Given her current situation, she'd thought wrong.

What *was* her current situation?

The cramped space was dark. But the darkness was neither uniform nor total, as she had first thought. She could make out a less dense square of darkness directly above her head. She reached for it. Her fingers bumped up against something smooth and cool. Glass-like.

Like a window through which some meager light was filtered.

A window in a box.

Because she was in a box. A metal box. If she stretched out her feet, her toes hit metal. If she extended her arms, her palms hit metal. A metal box with a window.

Oh, God, no.

She pressed her hands against the sides of the container and pushed as hard as she could, but she couldn't get leverage.

Her heart pounded.

She shoved her fingernails under the seam and pried. Her fingernails bent, split, and broke, but the lid didn't budge.

Cold sweat slicked her face as a wave of uncontrollable shaking wracked her limbs.

She was in a metal box with a window and a lid. She was in the iron coffin. Cassie's coffin.

Please, please don't let me be in here with Cassie.

She felt around in the gloom. No bones or peeling flesh. No rotting hair or clothing. No corpse.

Just her. Trapped in a coffin. Her heart galloped, and her breath came quick and shallow.

You have to hang on, she told herself.

*If you have a panic attack, you **will** die in here.*

Do the work.

First, she slowed her breathing. Deep breath in, two, three, four. Out, two, three, four.

In, two, three, four. Out, two, three, four.

In and out, until her breath was regular and slow.

Now relax your muscles, one by one. Start with your toes. Work all the way up, muscle by muscle. You control your body. Your body doesn't control you.

By the time she unclenched her jaw and relaxed her face, she was through it. She sagged against the coffin, wrung out from the effort. After a minute of rest, she made two fists with her hands.

"Help," she croaked.

She cried for help until her throat was dry, and she pounded on the lid until her hands were raw.

Nobody answered, nobody came.

odhi called the telephone number that Marvin Washington had scrawled on his business card. While he waited for the call to go through, he visualized the result he sought.

"Morning?" A groggy voice sounded in his ear.

"Marvin?"

"Yeah."

"This is Bodhi King. I apologize for the indecently early hour, but you did offer your assistance. Anytime. And I need it. Badly. Now."

"What can I do?" Marvin's voice was alert, ready. All traces of sleep erased. Once a soldier, always a soldier.

"The museum is closed today, right?"

"Yes, sir. We don't open on Sundays. Folks around

here take church seriously. And Sunday dinner afterward even more seriously."

"Perfect. I need to get into the museum."

He listened to Marvin's steady breathing while the security officer considered this request.

"Into Professor Jones' lab?"

He paused. Then, "No. Into Mrs. Sullivan's office."

Marvin let out a great whoosh of air but didn't respond.

"I can tell you why, but I think you'd rather not know."

"Is this related to Davina's murder?"

"I think so, yes."

Bodhi's throat went dry. His pulse ticked up. He needed Marvin's help if his idea had any chance of success.

Finally, in a mournful tone, Marvin said, "Ah . . . I'll meet you there in twenty minutes."

"Thank you. And Marvin, I have one more favor. Would you mind picking me up at the lodge on your way to the preserve?" If he could avoid involving Jason, he'd like to.

"Sure. Anything else? Maybe I should stop and pick you up coffee and a donut first?"

"Let's not be ridiculous. I'm a pathologist, not a cop."

The well-worn cops and donuts joke earned a small chuckle from Marvin. "See you in fifteen."

"I'll be waiting outside the gate."

Eliza was smart to meet her ride, whoever it had been, out of sight of the lodge. He could see no reason why he shouldn't also be smart.

He was leaning against one of the stacked stone pillars outside the gate when his phone vibrated. He pulled it from his pocket and checked the number of the incoming call on his display. Not Bette. Not Marvin. Not Eliza. Not Micah.

"This is Bodhi King."

"Dr. King, this is Detective Valtri. I'm calling at Chief Dexter's request. He asked me to let you know that Verna Martin is in custody for the murder of Davina Jones."

"Her cousin did it?"

"Yes, sir."

"Did she say why?"

Valtri's clipped tone didn't change. "Ms. Martin has not given a statement. And she's asserted her Fifth Amendment privilege against self-incrimination, so I don't expect an explanation any time soon, if ever."

"Then how—?"

"A neighbor of Davina's picked her out of a photo array. She told her husband that she had to stop at her cousin's house after work. And we've swabbed her cheek. Clive, our forensics guy, is pretty confident it'll be a match for evidence collected at the scene."

"Huh. Oh, did she happen to have a brooch on her when you picked her up?"

"Excuse me?"

"A fancy gold pin with a red stone?"

Valtri hesitated. "No. But—"

"Yes?"

"You didn't hear this from me, but according to her husband's statement, the reason she went to see Davina had something to do with jewelry. He said they were arguing over a necklace and maybe a pin, too."

"Huh. Thanks for the call."

"You're welcome."

"Wait—did the chief also ask you to call Bette Clark and Fred Bolton?"

"No, sir. I expect he'll tell them in person at the conference this morning."

"Right. Of course. Thanks again."

He clicked to end the call as a gray Volvo wagon pulled up. Marvin waved at him and popped the locks.

Bodhi settled into the passenger seat and warmed his hands in front of the hot air vent as Marvin headed down the road. He considered calling Bette with the news about Verna, but he didn't want to have to answer any questions about where he was or what he was doing. He'd text her after he took care of his business at the museum.

"Thanks for the lift."

"Sure. You want to warm your rear end? This thing has heated seats."

"No, I'm good, thanks. So I just got a call from the detective assigned to Davina's case. Thought you might like to know Verna's been charged with Davina's murder."

Marvin glanced away from the road. "For real?"

"For real."

"Hmph."

Bodhi agreed wholeheartedly.

They lapsed into a contemplative silence. After a moment, Marvin asked the question Bodhi knew was coming.

"So, do you still need to get into Mrs. Sullivan's office? Now that Verna's being charged and all?"

"I really do."

"And I still don't want to know why?"

"You really don't."

Marvin pursed his lips and lifted one hand from the wheel to scratch his neck. "Okay, then."

Bodhi exhaled quietly.

The station wagon rolled up to the preserve's entrance gate. Marvin dragged a hand across his face. He stared at the open gate.

"Something wrong?"

"This gate's supposed to be locked when the preserve and museum are closed. I locked it myself last night."

"So, someone else is here?"

"Evidently."

"That changes things."

"Unless they've come and gone already. Could've been one of the Sullivans."

"It's seven in the morning."

Marvin shrugged. "Only one way to find out."

He piloted the car through the open gate and followed the winding road through the preserve. The road wound around to the back of the museum building. There were no cars in the lot. He parked in a spot near the employee door.

They exited the Volvo, and he used his key fob to lock it remotely. Then he fished out the heavy ring of keys he'd used to unlock the lab yesterday and flipped through them until he found the one he wanted.

They walked into the cold, dark building, and Marvin turned on the main level lights. Their footsteps echoed sharply in the silence. Bodhi stooped and squinted at a small red splotch just inside the door.

"What is it?"

He looked up at Marvin. "It's blood." He reached into his jacket pocket and removed a sterile package of blue forensic gloves, ripped it open, and snapped them on.

He touched one fingertip to the spot. When he removed it, it was coated with red.

"And it's fresh."

Marvin reflexively reached toward his hip.

"You carrying?"

He nodded. "Sure am. You?"

"No," Bodhi said. "What's the play? Call the police?"

He hoped Marvin said no. He didn't want to have to explain his presence to Dexter or any of his officers.

Marvin thought for a moment, tilting his head from one direction to the other, and then said, "No. Let's sweep the building. Assuming we don't find anything concerning, you take care of whatever it is you need to do in Mrs. Sullivan's office. I'll take you back to the lodge and then call the police. There's no reason for you to be involved in this, whatever it is. And for all we know, it's a big fat heap of nothing."

It was the outcome he wanted. But he searched Marvin's face for signs of ambivalence. "Are you sure?"

"Yes. Come on."

They fell into a rhythm of quick steps as they walked in a circuit on each floor, checking each door that should have been locked to confirm that it was. They all were. And checking each door that should have been unlocked confirmed that it was. They all were, too. No lights were on that shouldn't have been. No materials were out of place. There was no sign of anything out of the ordinary, save the open front gate and a droplet of blood inside the door.

When they reached the top floor, they continued to clear each room with the same result and ended up in front of Margot Rutherford Sullivan's personal office.

Marvin eased the key into the lock, but before he turned it, he turned to Bodhi. "I'm going to go down the hallway and unlock the boardroom. I'm going take a peek in there. I'll be right back, okay?"

He walked off without waiting for Bodhi to answer. After he unlocked the boardroom doors and stepped inside—giving him plausible deniability, maybe— Bodhi twisted the knob and let himself into the inner sanctum.

He kept the forensic gloves on and the lights off. He walked directly to the photograph of Margot and Sully with the police chief and lifted it from the shelf. He held it one-handed and snapped a picture with his cell phone. Then he returned the framed photo to its spot and moved around to Margot's writing desk.

The small desk had a single drawer centered on the underside of the writing service. The drawer did not lock, which was not a surprise. A person in Margot Sullivan's position likely operated with complete conviction that her confidences would be kept, her privacy maintained. He eased open the drawer.

He found what he was looking for immediately and removed it. He dropped the familiar ornate ring into his pocket and closed the drawer. He strode back out into the hallway to wait for Marvin.

32

B odhi's phone rang before Marvin returned from the boardroom.

"Bette? Did you catch up with Eliza?"

"No." Her voice was strained.

"What happened?"

"We're at Davina's apartment waiting for Lew Dexter."

He stifled a groan. "You called Dexter? Why?"

"Because Eliza's not here, but Fred and I think she was." She dropped her voice. "There was nobody here when we got here. The crime scene technician and a uniformed officer had gone on a coffee run. They just got back. We ran into them in the lobby. The door was ajar, and there's blood on the floor outside Davina's bedroom."

"It was an exsanguination. She hemorrhaged and bled out. There was blood everywhere, Bette."

"It's not Davina's. We confirmed against the photographs Clive took yesterday that it's new. And—"

"—And it's fresh?" His legs threatened to give out, so he leaned against the wall for support.

"Yes. How did you guess?"

"As soon as Chief Dexter gets there, come over here."

"To the lodge?"

"What? No. The Rutherford Museum. In fact, maybe tell Dexter to meet you here and get one of the uniforms to drive you over. It'll be faster."

"What are you doing at the museum?"

"Long story. I'm here with the chief security officer. The gate was open when we arrived, and there was blood on the floor just inside the door. Not much, but enough that I noticed it. And it was—"

"Fresh," she finished in a voice laden with dread.

"Yeah."

"Well, the doer isn't Verna. Officer Kincaid just told us she's in custody."

"I heard. No, I think it's someone else connected to the museum, though."

"Okay. I'll bring Fred up to speed. We'll be there as fast as we can. And Bodhi—"

"Yeah?"

"Don't be a hero, please."

"Don't worry. Marvin, the security chief, is former military, and he's armed. I intend to do exactly what he says and nothing else."

"Excellent plan. Stay in one piece until I get there."

"Yes, Chief."

He ended the call just before the boardroom door opened and Marvin clomped out into the hall, whistling loudly. While Marvin locked up the boardroom, Bodhi hurried down the hall toward him.

"Find what you need?"

"Yes. Listen, that blood on the floor?"

"Yeah."

"It might be Eliza's. She was abducted from Davina's apartment this morning. I think they—whoever they are—brought her here."

Marvin's face went ashen. "We checked everywhere."

"We checked that all the doors were locked, or unlocked, as the case may be. We didn't check inside each room. But I don't think we have to. Let's start with the lab."

They raced to the stairwell.

33

E liza's forehead throbbed. She tried to shift onto her side. If she could prop herself on her hip and elevate her head, it would help to alleviate some of the pressure. But she was much taller than Cassie had been in life, and the coffin was too cramped to allow for maneuvering. She made it about a quarter turn, then conceded defeat and returned to her back.

She stared up at the dim square of gray light afforded by the window, wondering how much time had passed. Her eyes burned from straining in the darkness. Her chest and lungs ached from the lack of fresh air. And she was getting sleepy. She was certain falling asleep in the coffin meant dying in the coffin.

This thought kicked off a new wave of panic,

which she had to beat back, leaving her more drained, more exhausted. Tears would have filled her eyes if she hadn't been so dehydrated.

Make a decision, she told herself. *Fight or submit. But whatever you're gonna do, commit to it and do it already.*

She was awfully tired.

But Fred would be destroyed if she died, especially like this. It really *was* a horrible way to die, and she'd seen all kinds of gruesome, heartbreaking, and tragic deaths, so she felt qualified to judge it. She really *didn't* want to die.

But, wow, was she tired.

Could she possibly hold on until someone found her?

Another question crowded in on her, threatening to overwhelm her and suffocate her, but she pushed it away. She couldn't give in to that fear. Still, the question was there, looming in the gathering tenebrosity:

What if her attacker returned to finish her off?

Bodhi had never understood the phrase '*my heart was in my throat.*' From a purely anatomical standpoint, it was, of course, impossible. And even as a descriptor of terror or dread, it had always struck him as melodramatic, verging on histrionic.

But, as he waited for Marvin to unlock the door to Davina's laboratory, he felt as if his heart were in his throat. The tightness of his throat and his thudding pulse tricked his brain into believing that he could not breathe, so now his breaths came fast, frantic.

He keyed into his heartbeat and tied his inhalations and exhalations to its wild, choppy rhythm in the hopes of slowing it and calming himself. Marvin turned the key in the lock, and Bodhi prepared himself to accept whatever they might find inside.

Marvin pushed the door open. It creaked, and the sound was straight out of a horror film. They walked into the cold room, and Marvin turned on the lights.

Marvin scanned the room. "I don't see anything out of place."

Bodhi nodded. At first glance, neither did he. He scanned the floor first. No visible blood. No signs of a struggle in the tidy work area. Cassie still rested on the table where he and Eliza had left her. "Wait."

"What is it?"

"Yesterday, the three of us removed the lid from the coffin and set it aside."

Marvin followed his gaze. The lid covered the coffin.

"You and Dr. Rollins didn't put that back on before you left?"

"No. It was heavy, and we figured we'd be returning Cassie, er, the body, to the coffin sooner rather than later, so we left it as it was."

"But the body's not in the coffin."

"Nope, it's not."

He approached the table warily. The lid was lined up perfectly with no gaps between the coffin and the cover. He peered down into the window. Eliza stared back up at him. Her eyes were enormous, and dried blood covered most of the top of her forehead and parts of her face.

For one endless heartbeat, he was sure she was dead. Then her mouth opened in an almost-silent scream. "Get me out of here," she croaked softly.

"Marvin!" Bodhi shouted, but the security officer was already at his side.

They each gripped an end of the coffin lid and heaved. Preservation of a historically significant object was the furthest thing from their minds. The lid clattered to the floor with a tremendous crash that echoed off the tile walls.

Eliza pushed herself up to her elbows, panting and shaking.

"Stay still. We've got you."

He and Marvin lifted her from the coffin, supporting her on either side. There were no chairs in the room, so they lowered her to a seated position on the metal table with her legs dangling over its edge. She wrapped her fingers around the table's lip with a white-knuckled grip and swallowed down the fresh air in greedy gulps.

"May I have a look?" Bodhi gestured toward her forehead.

She turned her face up to the ceiling so he'd have a better angle from which to assess her wound. "It probably looks worse than it is."

"Lucky that it caught you on the forehead rather than the temple. That may have saved your life."

She showed no signs of having heard him.

"When I came to, I was in the coffin. I thought I was going to die in there."

She shivered, whether from the cold or the memory, Bodhi couldn't tell. He took off his jacket and draped it over her shoulders.

Marvin crouched in front of her. "Can I get you something, Doc? Maybe a glass of water?"

She nodded her head. "Please."

"I'll be right back with it."

"Chief Dexter ought to be here any minute. Will you keep an eye out for him?" Bodhi asked.

"Sure thing."

As soon as Marvin closed the door behind him, Eliza reached behind her neck with both hands.

She fumbled for a second, then said, "My hands are too shaky. Help me with this."

She bent her head down to expose the silver clasp at the back of her neck.

He unhooked it. "Is this—?"

"Yes. I went to Davina's this morning and found her jewelry box."

He lifted the necklace out from under her shirt and studied the filigree pattern and the brilliant-cut stone. "They're all the same."

"Both the same, you mean."

He shook his head. "The reason Marvin and I are here is that I was looking for something in Margot Sullivan's office."

"What?"

He reached into his pants pocket and removed the ring he'd taken from Margot's desk drawer. "This."

She stared at the ring in his right hand, and then at the necklace in his left. "I don't understand."

"Neither do I, really. But they're all the same pattern, the same stone. They're connected."

"How did you know to look for that?" She gestured at the ring.

"Yesterday, when I was looking at her photographs, it caught my eye. She's wearing it in all of them. But the picture of her getting that award from the chief really shows the details. I thought it was similar to the brooch Davina photographed. But I wasn't positive it was the same. Then I remembered her fingers."

"Whose fingers?"

"Margot's. When we were introduced, she shook my hand . . . Sort of. She extended the fingers of her right hand, holding it out, palm-down, parallel to the floor. So I shook them as best I could. She was wearing a large, heavy ring on her right index finger, and two rings on her left hand, but nothing on her right ring finger."

"Okay, so?"

"So that's the one the ring was on in all the pictures. And the finger itself is noticeably thinner at the bottom. Likely worn down from wearing that ring for decades. Why take it off now?"

"To hide the connection."

"Bingo."

"So you broke into the museum to look for it."

"Once we realized you went to Davina's, I figured you'd gone to find her necklace. So, yeah, why not go for the trifecta?"

The color had been returning to Eliza's face, but now she blanched. "You just said 'we.' Fred knows?"

"He woke up, and you were gone. Long story short, he and Bette headed to Davina's to find you. They told me to wait at the lodge. Oops." He shrugged.

A faint smile bloomed on her lips. "Maybe we're both the bad influence."

"It's possible. But, on a serious note, he walked into a bad scene. Your blood was all over the floor, along with the weapon. And you were nowhere to be found. They're on their way here, too. He's out of his mind with worry."

She nodded. "How did you and Marvin know to look for me in here?"

"The gates were open when we got here, and they shouldn't have been. Nothing else was out of place except for a small amount of fresh blood just inside the door. We didn't think that much of it at first. Then Bette called and told me what had happened at Davina's apartment and that you were missing."

"I can't stop thinking about what would have happened if you hadn't been here."

He rubbed her shoulder. "You're okay. You should get your forehead looked at to be sure, but you're okay."

"Thanks for saving my life . . . for the second time."

"You're welcome. But I'm not keeping count."

She smiled, and the smile reached her eyes. "Well, I am. So, what do we do now?"

"I guess we wait and see what Chief Dexter wants to do."

"Yippee."

He knew the feeling.

34

Marvin returned with Eliza's water—and Margot Rutherford Sullivan, who instantly took charge of the room.

"What on earth is going on here? Mr. Washington tells me that Dr. Rollins was assaulted. Do we need to call for an ambulance?" She frowned at Eliza's bloodied face. "Oh dear."

Eliza shook her head, winced, then groaned. After she caught her breath, she said, "I'll get checked out later."

She took several greedy gulps of the water Marvin provided.

"Hey, slow down. You were in there for several hours. Don't overwhelm your system," Bodhi warned her.

"In where?" Margot said to Bodhi in an undertone.

"The iron coffin. She's lucky she survived."

Margot blanched but recovered quickly. "And how did you happen to be here? The museum is closed. I was just coming in to do some administrative work when I ran into Mr. Washington."

He studied her face. "I think it's time to give up the ghost, don't you?"

"I beg your pardon?"

"I have your ring and Davina's necklace. They're a set."

"My ring? You stole my ring?"

"I borrowed your ring to confirm a theory. I'm guessing whoever takes over for Chief Dexter will forgive me since they'll be able to clear a murder and an attempted murder within the first hour of their tenure."

Eliza turned to them and wrinkled her brow. "What do you mean? You know who did this to me?"

"Sure. So does Mrs. Sullivan. It was her grandson. With a little help from his friendly neighborhood police chief."

"I beg your pardon?"

"Are you sure about this, Dr. King?" Marvin wanted to know.

"Pretty sure."

The security guard frowned. "Is there anyone at the station who you trust? I'd rather not have Chief Dexter show up here armed and looking for a fight if we can avoid it."

"Smart man. I don't know for sure, but I think the rot is limited to the chief. Detective Valtri springs to mind."

"I'll call and ask her to get over here ASAP."

"Thanks, Marvin."

He nodded and left the room. Bodhi hit his speakerphone button and dialed Bette's number. She answered immediately.

"We're on our way. We're just outside the entrance to the preserve. Some idiot wrapped his BMW around a tree and it's blocking the . . ."

Margot clutched her chest. "What color is the vehicle?"

"Did you hear that, Bette?"

"Uh, yeah. It's silver. Why?"

Margot swayed and grabbed on to the wall for support.

Bodhi kept an eye on her to make sure she didn't collapse while he answered. "I'm guessing it's Sully's car. Is the driver injured?"

"He took off, actually. Into the woods that lead back to the lodge."

"Do you and Fred feel up to a cross-country run?"

"Ah, crap. Really?"

"I'm almost positive he killed Davina. And I think he and Dexter worked together to attack and abduct Eliza. Tell Fred she's okay, by the way. I mean, a little worse for wear. But in one piece."

"Love you, Fred," Eliza called hoarsely.

"I'll deliver that message. See you soon."

"Run like the wind." He ended the call and turned to face Margot.

"What the devil is going on?" she demanded.

"Where's the brooch?" he responded.

"What business is that of yours?" She'd recovered from her initial shock and had drawn herself up. She was the perfect well-bred lady again.

"Well, it doesn't belong to you. It belongs to her." He nodded toward Cassie's corpse.

Margot huffed through her nose. "*She* is Alice Catherine Rutherford. She's my great, great, great-aunt. So, I feel justified in laying claim to the jewelry that was stolen off her corpse by Professor Jones."

"If you knew who she was, why didn't you tell Davina?" Eliza asked.

"Because it was none of her business. Just as it's none of yours."

"You don't care that your aunt was hanged?" Bodhi couldn't help himself. The words just popped out.

"You know she doesn't. Only pretty history, remember?" Eliza must've been feeling better. Or her adrenaline had overwhelmed her fatigue. Either way, her eyes blazed.

"That's not how it is," Margot insisted.

"You're the last living Rutherford woman. Or at least you are now. When you and Davina saw the brooch, she knew it matched her necklace, and you knew it matched your ring."

She sniffed.

"But you had the advantage because you knew what it meant. She didn't."

"Care to fill me in?" Eliza asked.

"It's how the Rutherford women established lineage and the right to take under the trust. Right, Mrs. Sullivan?"

She exhaled. "Yes. Louisa Anne Rutherford established the trust and used a set of jewelry that her late husband had made for her to identify the original beneficiaries. The pin went to Alice, who mustn't have had any female children, because, as we know, it was buried with her. The ring went to Alice's only sister Deborah and was handed down through female children as follows: Deborah to Caroline to Eloise to

Charlotte to me. I had two sons, both of whom are deceased, and my younger boy Paul had Eugene. So that's the end of the line for the ring. I suppose I'll be wearing it when I'm buried." She rubbed her empty finger with an absent gesture.

"So, how did Davina end up with the necklace?" Eliza asked.

"I have no idea," Margot responded.

They both turned to Bodhi. "I'm not sure. But I bet Micah Birch knows something. My phone's been blowing up for the last hour with texts and calls from him."

"Why didn't you answer?"

"We've been a bit busy here."

"Fair point."

35

Sully and Dexter were taken into custody without incident thanks to Bette's fleet feet and Detective Valtri's quick draw.

Once the excitement died down, Marvin unlocked the doors to the board room and ushered Bodhi, Eliza, Bette, and Fred inside.

Margot Rutherford Sullivan sat at the far end of the table. She looked like a pale replica of herself.

"You sure you don't want to go to the hospital?" Marvin asked Eliza.

"Later. I don't want to miss Micah's presentation."

Marvin shook his head. "Mr. Birch should be here any minute. Anybody want anything else before he gets here?"

Margot gestured toward the coffee, tea, and water

that Marvin had procured as if by magic. "I think we're covered, Mr. Washington. Thank you."

Marvin nodded and started for the door.

"I thought you were a history buff. Don't you want to stay and hear Micah lay out the whole story?" Bodhi asked.

Joy lit Marvin's eyes. "I really kind of do."

"Pull up a chair," Fred boomed, his arm draped over Eliza's shoulder. Eliza rested her head on his chest.

Marvin took the seat next to Bette just as Micah appeared in the doorway.

"Hi. That officer down at the front door—Kincaid? He said to just come on up. I hope that's okay?"

"It's perfect," Bodhi said.

Micah walked into the room and rested a weathered leather briefcase on the gleaming conference table.

"It sounds like you've had an exciting day already," he began. "But buckle up."

He opened the bag and laid out photocopies of several letters. "So we were off by about a decade. Alice Catherine Rutherford died in 1871. She hanged herself."

"It was a suicide," Eliza breathed.

"She hanged herself because she had been

working with Isaiah Bell to set up a school for free blacks, and the two of them fell in love."

"Star-crossed lovers?" Marvin asked.

"And then some. The Rutherfords were wealthy and influential. They were also sympathetic to the plight of the newly emancipated slaves."

"Scalawags?" Bodhi remembered Davina's explanation.

"Up to a point. They were Southern Republicans, and they supported Isaiah's bid for Congress. But when they found out he was sleeping with their daughter . . . that was another story entirely."

Margot dropped her eyes to the table.

Micah went on, "It looks like they intercepted a letter from Alice to Isaiah arranging a meeting. They used to meet up at his cousin's farm, under the tree where Davina found the coffin."

He spread out several more letters, poured himself a glass of water, and then continued, "In July of 1871, Isaiah arrived at the designated spot to find, not his beloved, but her shotgun-toting father. A month later, he was living in Wales."

"And that's why Alice killed herself?" Bette hypothesized. "She thought he dumped her?"

Micah frowned sadly. "Worse. She was pregnant with Isaiah's baby. Once he left town without so much as a see-ya-later, she was too hurt to try to send him word. The Rutherfords were scandalized. After she had the child . . ." He trailed off and passed around copies of Alice and Isaiah's correspondence.

"Anyway, the Rutherfords gave the baby away. It's all in the last letter from Alice to Isaiah. She sent it, and then she hanged herself from the black cherry tree on Jonah's farm."

A thick silence blanketed the room.

Finally, Marvin said, "How does the necklace come into play?"

"Alice killed herself the first week of December, so the baby was likely born in November. Alice must've somehow made sure the necklace went with the baby. Maybe she wrapped it in the blanket or tucked it in a diaper. I don't know. But somehow, she made sure her daughter got part of her inheritance."

Comprehension dawned and spread across the room.

"Wait, Davina was right? She was related to Isaiah Bell?" Bodhi asked.

"Isaiah and Alice. I'm still running this down, but in one of her letters, Alice mentions a former attendant named Rebekah."

Margot cleared her throat. "Rebekah Truth. She's in the family records. And I don't think Alice gave the piece to the baby. That would most likely have been Louisa Anne, securing the baby's claim to the trust. There were always whispers, but never anything concrete."

Just then, Officer Kincaid stuck his head into the room. "Sorry to interrupt, but Detective Valtri wanted me to let you know Eugene Sullivan's cooperating. He'll admit his part and testify against Dexter in exchange for a quiet plea deal. He says he doesn't want to embarrass his grandmother any more than he already has."

Margot closed her eyes and exhaled through her nose. When she regained her hold on her emotions and opened her eyes, Bodhi asked, "Do you have any idea why he killed Davina?"

She paused for half a minute before answering.

"He lacks the imagination to picture a life without the trust, without his status and his allowance. I blame myself. I told him to go talk to Davina. I wanted him to convince her to handle her claim, to the extent she had one, in a private manner. I think he saw an opportunity to remove her claim entirely and took it. With her dead, he likely thought I'd give in to his incessant requests to amend the trust."

She lifted her chin. "But what Eugene didn't understand is that I would never do that."

"Why not?" Bette asked. "If it was in your power?"

"Because the foundation was never about me. Or him. It was about Louisa Anne's vision. My job was to see it through. I've made a mess of it, obviously. But I would never turn away from it."

She buried her face in her hands. She cried soundlessly, her shaking shoulders the only evidence of her distress.

36

Sunday evening
Impromptu Q and A Session with Chief Clark and Chief
Bolton Regarding Corruption in a Small-Town Department

Bodhi and Eliza tiptoed into the standing room only session and pressed themselves against the back wall to listen to Bette and Fred field questions about the case from over a hundred excited police chiefs.

Eliza leaned over and whispered, "Did you hear about Verna?"

"Part of it. I guess Verna did go to Davina's apartment that afternoon, and she ran into Sully coming out of the building on her way in."

"Yeah. I doubt he recognized her, but she knew him. He did notice the museum parking permit on her car and called to ask Marvin to run the plate."

"So he could frame her?"

"Apparently. It was pretty clever, actually. But once Marvin gave his statement, Detective Valtri went back to the neighbor who made the bad identification. She folded like a piece of paper."

"Sully bribed her?"

"Nope. Dexter threatened her with a drug charge. She says he planted the drugs in her place."

"He just gets dirtier and dirtier," Bodhi remarked.

"He must've really wanted Sully to take control of the foundation."

"Oh, I did hear one thing from Bette. Detective Valtri set the Chinese delivery guy up with a sketch artist and had him describe the man he saw in the lobby."

"Sully?"

"Sully."

"Poor Verna. She almost went down for murder." She clicked her tongue against her teeth in sympathy.

"As far as I can tell, Sully wasn't really even trying

to frame her for that. He just wanted to be able to give his grandmother a story about how he got the brooch from Davina's apartment. Dexter's the one who realized Verna was the perfect patsy for Davina's murder."

"So, Margot knew he'd been to the apartment. That's why they hurried us out of there when we asked if they had alibis."

"Yeah. She *claims* she didn't tell us because she believed Sully's story about running into Verna and leaving without seeing Davina. I guess she figured why be truthful and risk being dragged into a scandal." Bodhi suppressed a sigh.

"Having gotten to know these people, does any of this surprise you?"

"Actually, no," he admitted.

Just then, a tall, thin man wearing a tweed blazer popped to his feet. "This question is for Chief Bolton. Fred, I hear Lewis Dexter participated in the abduction of your . . . uh, girlfriend. Is that true?"

Fred nodded. "Well, Tony, Dexter isn't talking. But the uniformed officers who were guarding the scene confirm he's the one who sent them away on an errand so that his co-conspirator, Eugene Sullivan, could access the scene. Sullivan is cooperating. He claims that after he attacked Dr. Rollins, he called Dexter for help. Dexter met him at the front gate of the museum and helped him carry Dr. Rollins, who was unconscious and bleeding, into the building and stuff her into a coffin . . ." His voice cracked.

Bette jumped in. "So, you can connect the dots yourself, Tony. Suffice it to say, Lewis Dexter was into this up to his neck."

Eliza leaned over again. "Fred and I are leaving tonight."

"Not sticking around until tomorrow?"

"No, we have to get back. We're actually taking off right after this session. So, if I don't see . . . well, thanks."

"Please stop thanking me."

She grinned. "Nope."

"In that case, you're welcome. Let's hope the next time we meet up, it's not at a conference."

She pulled a face. "It'll probably be to testify."

He nodded. "Probably."

"That's okay. I've decided I hate conferences."

Bodhi didn't try to hide his grin.

They turned their attention back to the questions being lobbed at Fred and Bette for a while.

After a few moments, Eliza whispered, "I don't want to hear anymore. I'm going to go check out so we can leave as soon as he finishes up. You take care of yourself, okay?"

"Yeah. You, too."

"And Bodhi? Leave the past in the past. You'll be happier if you do." She picked up her bag and edged her way out of the room.

37

Huntsville, December 2, 1871

Dear Isaiah,

I hear you are still abroad. How lovely for you. I trust you are well.

I am not.

I would say I have my memories to console me, but it would be a lie. My memories torment me. And it is a torment I cannot bear.

The past is one sort of torture, and the thought of the future another. I think of what might have been and what will never be. And I cannot feel any hope or any happiness.

Farewell,

Alice

Monday morning

Bodhi and Bette said their goodbyes sitting on the same glider in the same gazebo where they'd stargazed only a few nights earlier. It felt like it had been years, though.

Her flight was scheduled to depart hours earlier than his. He'd imagined they'd share a ride to the airport anyway, and he'd hang out there and wait. But she'd said no.

The 'no,' really told him everything he needed to know. But he sensed that it was important to her to speak her piece, so here they were.

The glider creaked. *Forward, back. Forward, back.*

Bette sighed and stood up.

He stopped the glider's movement with his feet and waited.

She stared at him, dry-eyed but sad. "Here's the deal. I don't care about your past. And I don't even really care about our future. But I *do* care about the present, the now. Us. And for all your Buddhisting about mindfulness and presence, it doesn't feel like it matters to you. Or at least not enough."

"Bette, I—"

"Please don't. Just let me say what I need to say. I'm supposed to leave for the airport in five minutes."

He clamped his mouth shut.

She gave him a wan smile. "Thanks. I want to be with you. Now. Without your worrying about whether it's right action to have sex with me unless you first tell me every crappy thing you did in college or med school. Without your wondering whether it's right speech to let me know it drives you bonkers when I leave cabinet doors hanging open. When—if—you're ready for a real relationship, with all the messiness and imperfection that entails, you know where to find me."

She turned and glanced at the driveway, where Jason waited, engine idling. Her bags were already in the trunk of the car.

Her words were a gut punch. He sat there for a moment and absorbed it all. Then he stood.

"Can I say goodbye?"

She nodded mutely.

He hugged her tight and smoothed her hair while she wrapped her arms around his neck.

"I'm sorry," he whispered.

"I know," she mumbled into his throat. "Me, too."

And then, she gently pulled away and walked toward the waiting car. She didn't turn around.

He lowered himself back on to the glider and creaked, *forward, back, forward, back,* until Jason returned hours later to tell him they had to leave if he was going to make his flight.

38

Six weeks later
Rutherford Nature Preserve and Open-Air Museum
Jonah Bell Historical Site and Rutherford-Jones Memorial

M icah led Bodhi past the cabin and the active dig site to the memorial.

"I thought it should be here, under the black cherry tree, because the spot meant something to both Davina and Alice," Micah explained.

They stared down at the marble stone's inscription together:

ALICE CATHERINE RUTHERFORD (1849-1871)
DAVINA TRUTH JONES (1988-2020)

*History is a set of lies that people have agreed upon. Even
when I am gone, I shall remain in people's minds the star of
their rights, my name will be the war cry of their efforts,
the motto of their hopes.*
Napoleon Bonaparte

"Interesting choice for an epitaph," Bodhi observed without turning away from the small monument.

"Margot chose it."

He cocked his head and turned to Micah. "Margot Sullivan?"

"Yeah. She paid, so she picked it. I did point out that Napoleon himself credited Voltaire with coinage, but she insisted."

"It's hard to picture her visiting her grandson in prison," Bodhi mused.

Micah scoffed. "Come on, man. She's Margot Rutherford Sullivan. Sully's out on bond. He does have to wear an ankle bracelet, though."

"Figures."

"Margot is trying to make amends, though. She's

accepted that she can't whitewash history. And she donated her ring and Alice's brooch to the archives."

"Wow. Wait—what about Davina's necklace?"

"That one's in legal limbo, I guess. Verna might have a claim to it after all. If not, it'll always have a home with the archives. Really, those pieces belong here, but the history is ... complicated."

"And how's your joint project with the Rutherford Museum going?"

"It's promising. Bringing the relationship between Alice and Isaiah to light is a big deal. And having a partner at the Rutherford Museum who's committed to not pulling any punches has made it really exciting. We're going to tell the whole story—their love affair, the baby, Alice's suicide, and Isaiah's depression and self-exile. It's going to be meaty."

"Who's your counterpart at the Sullivan? I assume Margot and Sully are a bit preoccupied with his legal problems."

A broad grin split Micah's face. "Believe it or not, Marvin Washington stepped up to fill the void. Turns out that guy loves history." He glanced at his watch. "In fact, I have a meeting with him to discuss the potential of having the archives absorb the museum."

"Really?"

"Yeah, Margot plans to let the foundation dissolve on her death unless another female Rutherford turns up. We'd be interested in taking over the grounds and the assets. But it's complicated."

"I can only imagine."

"I do have to run. But you should stay as long as you like."

They shook hands.

"I'm just passing through. I had a layover in Huntsville and plenty of time, so I wanted to drop by and pay my respects."

"Where are you headed?"

"I'm going to see Bette in Illinois."

"Things are good?"

"Things are . . . complicated, but good."

Micah nodded, apparently satisfied with the cryptic answer, and strode across the lawn to the museum. Bodhi stayed where he was.

Things were complicated. And they were good.

He bowed his head over Alice and Davina's final resting place and closed his eyes to wish them peace. Then he pulled out his phone to let Jason know he was ready to return to the airport.

He was ready.

Ready to stop chasing after the past.

Ready to stop placing expectations on the future.

Ready to take each day as it came with a clear-eyed vision of the present, even if that meant telling Bette it drove him bonkers when she left the cabinet doors hanging open.

AUTHOR'S NOTE

Most of my Bodhi King novels are sparked by an astonishing scientific fact I stumble across. Not this one. I got the idea to write Cold Path while on a family RV trip.

Our destination was the U.S. Space and Rocket Center in Huntsville, Alabama (which, by the way, is fascinating!). We stayed way up in the mountains at Monte Sano State Park, which has miles of hiking trails, great stargazing, and friendly deer and is home to the Northern Alabama Japanese Garden.

As soon as I set foot in the garden, Bodhi's destiny was sealed—he was coming to Alabama.

There's a historical museum just down the mountain from the state park. We didn't visit it. (After a few overzealous excursions, my kids have imposed limits on how many museums, art galleries, and science centers I can drag them to in a day.) But, wheels were turning.

Then I read an article about iron coffins, and we were off to the races! I can't remember which article sparked the idea, but here's a handful of sources (from least to most academic) that will give you a flavor:

"The Cast Iron Coffin That Was Too Creepy Even for the Victorians," Allison Meier, Atlas Obscura (December 30, 2013)

"Iron Coffin Protected Century Old Life Story," Boyce Rensberger, The Washington Post (April 9, 1988)

"The Man in the Iron Coffin: An Interdisciplinary Effort to Name the Past," Douglas W. Owsley, Karin S. Bruwelheide, Larry W. Cartmell, Sr., Laurie E.Burgess, Shelly J. Foote, Skye M. Chang and Nick Fielder, Historical Archaeology, Vol. 40, No. 3, Remains of the Day: Forensic Applications in Archaeology (2006), pp. 89-108.

There's also an episode of Secrets of the Dead: Unearthing History, titled "The Woman in the Iron Coffin," which you can stream from PBS if you really want to learn about iron coffins!

So, with a dead body dating back to the mid-1800s, it was time to do some historical research!

The character of Isaiah Matthew Bell is fictional, but I drew inspiration from these real-life Reconstruction Era African-American lawmakers from Alabama: Benjamin S. Turner; James T. Rapier; Jeremiah Haralson; and William Hooper Councill.

There's no way I can do justice to any of these men with a sentence or two, so please check out their short bios on the Alabama Humanities Foundation and Auburn University's joint venture, the Encyclopedia of Alabama site, to learn about them at www.encyclopediaofalabama.org.

Lynchings were common in the South, and the victims were overwhelmingly black. These materials some horrific descriptions and images, so please proceed with caution if you read them.

"Lynching in America: Confronting the Legacy of Racial Terror," Equal Justice Initiative Report (3rd edition)

"History of Lynchings," NAACP web page

So-called scalawags, carpetbaggers, and sympathetic Southern Republicans were threatened by the KKK and targeted with violence.

"A Prospective Scene in the 'City of Oaks,' 4th March 1896," political cartoon, Tuscaloosa Independent Monitor (September 1, 1868)

"The Role of the Scalawag in Alabama Reconstruction," Sarah Van voorhis Woolfolk, dissertation thesis, Louisiana State University and Agricultural & Mechanical College (1965).

So, there you have it. Cold Path was inspired by a walk through a Japanese Zen garden.

HANG ON, DON'T I RECOGNIZE SOME OF THESE PEOPLE?

Yes, probably! The characters in my Bodhi King

Forensic Thriller Series, Sasha McCandless Legal Thriller Series, and Aroostine Higgins Thriller Series all live in the same universe. So, from time to time, they will pop up in one another's books, just like when you run into a neighbor at the grocery store or a coworker at your dentist's office.

It's on my list to create a comprehensive list or map of these times when my characters run into each other. (Some day!)

For now, the characters in Cold Path who've appeared in other series are Eliza Rollins and Fred Bolton, who we meet in Calculated Risk (Aroostine Higgins No. 3).

And, as a second degree of separation, Bodhi and Aroostine go way back. All the way back to Sasha and Leo's wedding in A Marriage of True Minds: A Sasha McCandless Novella (No. 2), where both Bodhi and Aroostine are guests at the ill-fated destination wedding turned hostage event.

Bodhi also appears in Improper Influence (Sasha McCandless Legal Thriller No. 5) and The Humble Salve: A Sasha McCandless Novella (No. 4).

And Aroostine pops up at the end of Inadvertent Disclosure (Sasha McCandless Legal Thriller No. 2) and Indispensable Party (Sasha McCandless Legal Thriller No. 4), as well as A Marriage of True Minds: A Sasha McCandless Novella (No. 2).

It's an eventful shared universe, what can I say?

THANK YOU!

Thanks for reading *Cold Path!* Bodhi will be back in another adventure soon. While you wait, you can always find an up-to-date list of the titles in this series, as well as my other books, on my website, www.melissafmiller.com.

Sign up. To be the first to know when I have a new release, sign up for my email newsletter. Prefer text alerts? Text BOOKS to 636-303-1088 to receive new release alerts and updates. Subscribers receive new release alerts, notices of sales and other book news, goodies, and exclusive subscriber bonuses.

Keep reading. Check out the first book in one (or all) of my other three series:

Irreparable Harm (Sasha McCandless Legal Thriller No. 1):

Sasha's a five-foot nothing attorney who's trained in Krav Maga. She's smart, funny, and utterly fearless. More than one million readers agree: you wouldn't want to face off against her in court ... or in a dark alley.

Critical Vulnerability (Aroostine Higgins Thriller No. 1):

Aroostine relies on her Native American traditions and her legal training to right wrongs and dispense justice. She's charmingly relentless, always dots her *i*'s and crosses her *t*'s, and is an expert tracker.

Rosemary's Gravy (We Sisters Three Humorous Romantic Mystery No. 1):

Rosemary, Sage, and Thyme are three twenty-something sisters searching for career success and love. Somehow, though, they keep finding murder and mayhem ... and love.

Share it. If you liked this book, please lend your copy to a friend who might enjoy it.

Review it. Please consider posting a short review. Honest reader reviews help others decide whether they'll enjoy a book.

ALSO BY MELISSA F. MILLER

The Sasha McCandless Legal Thriller Series

Irreparable Harm

Inadvertent Disclosure

Irretrievably Broken

Indispensable Party

Lovers and Madmen (Novella)

Improper Influence

A Marriage of True Minds (Novella)

Irrevocable Trust

Irrefutable Evidence

A Mingled Yarn (Novella)

Informed Consent

International Incident

Imminent Peril

The Humble Salve (Novella)

Intentional Acts

In Absentia

The Aroostine Higgins Novels

Critical Vulnerability

Chilling Effect

Calculated Risk

Called Home

Crossfire Creek

The Bodhi King Novels

Dark Path

Lonely Path

Hidden Path

Twisted Path

Cold Path

The We Sisters Three Romantic Comedic Mysteries

Rosemary's Gravy

Sage of Innocence

Thyme to Live

Lost and Gowned: Rosemary's Wedding

Wedding Bells and Hoodoo Spells: Sage's Wedding

Wanted Wed or Alive: Thyme's Wedding

Made in United States
North Haven, CT
14 September 2022

24092140R00200